Saint: Sin City MC Oakland Chapter

Courtney Dean

CHAPTER ONE

Forbidden Ink

A knock sounded at the door, and I killed the gun. Snake cursed under his breath. "Motherfucker, how much longer?"

"You want it done right, Snake?" He responded with a mumble. "Fucking asshole."

We'd been at this shit since this morning, and Snake was a grumpy, impatient motherfucker. He loved getting tattooed but hated sitting for them. I was used to his complaining ass. He sponsored me when I prospected for the club against the wishes of both of my brothers. And he'd been an asshole for as long as I'd known him.

"Yeah!" I called out to Angel through the closed door.

It was Sunday. Angel and I were the only ones at the shop tonight. The crew chose whether they wanted to take Sundays off or work. If they did come in, it was for the morning clients or appointments. Rarely did walk-ins show up.

Angel was our receptionist. He was an ex-con and the half-brother of a friend. He hated when we called him our receptionist. The term wasn't manly enough for his sexist ass. He liked to call himself the fucking gatekeeper. Every time he said that shit, I couldn't do anything but laugh.

Angel pushed the door open and leaned against the frame of the door like he was posing for a magazine cover. All the women loved him despite his criminal past. He was great at attracting new female customers. He looked like some actor from one of those biker shows on television that didn't know shit about being a one-percenter. And he loved the attention. Despite his high opinion of himself, he was perfect for the position.

"You got a walk-in." He popped a piece of mint candy in his mouth. He didn't go anywhere without' em.

"Son of a bitch," I groaned causing a smirk to cross his face. "I was fucking hoping I could make it out of here before anyone showed up."

Everybody knew I hated walk-ins. It was usually a drunk college kid who wanted to get his girlfriend's name tattooed across his ass to show his undying love. Or a drunk girl whining about how her boyfriend cheated on her and she wanted to get a tattoo to mark the occasion of when she dumped him. Not how I liked to spend my time or waste my talent. Of course, I hated to lose money, but we were one of the few shops that didn't tattoo drunk people.

I also tattooed by appointment only, unless it was one of the brothers, or on one of these days when no one else was in the shop like tonight. My waitlist was one to two months long and I worked seven days a week. For me, it was hard to squeeze in walk-ins, so when I didn't have an appointment, my free time was reserved for the brothers. However, money was money and today I didn't have a choice. I was the only one here.

"Give me ten minutes," I grumbled.

"You got it, boss," he said, shutting the door behind him.

"Almost done, brother," I said to calm Snake's ornery ass.

"Thank fuck!" he groaned as he laid back in the tattoo chair, getting comfortable.

It took almost the entire day to finish the sleeve on his forearm. We'd been working on it since ten this morning, with minimal breaks and no lunch. Once we got started on his pieces, he hated to take breaks. And now, both of us were ready for the shit to be done.

"Shit hurts like a motherfucker," he growled, pulling on his long gray beard with his free hand. "And my ass is numb."

"You're the motherfucker who didn't want to take a break, Snake. So, stop fucking complaining now."

"Fuck you, Saint," he grumbled.

He knew I was right. I chuckled and restarted the tattoo gun. The constant buzzing of the machine always brought me peace. I relaxed and slipped back into the zone. As I finished the shading on the dripping fangs of the cobra coiling around Snake's huge ass forearm, the tension of the long day ebbed away, but tiredness set in. While I loved creating art and wouldn't want to do anything else, I was fucking tired. After long days at the shop and other days spent on runs for Sin City, I was burned out. All I wanted was to go home, smoke a joint, and pass the fuck out for a few days.

I shaded the last drip of venom and breathed a sigh of relief when it was done, then I shut the gun off.

"All done." I sprayed the area on his arm and wiped away the excess ink from his skin. "Tell me what you think."

Snake slid off the leather chair and stood in front of the large mirror hanging on the wall. Ink covered him from head to toe. Even crosses were tattooed on his eyelids. He wasn't opposed to getting ink anywhere. And he knew good art when he saw it. What Snake thought of my work mattered to me, like all my brothers. Although I wouldn't tell them or Snake that shit because I'd never hear the end of it. He was one of the older members of Sin City and had paid his dues to the club. He also had been tattooed by some of the greats in the field, including my mentor.

"That shit looks real good kid." He twisted his muscular arm from side to side, inspecting the detailed black and white tattoo. "Real fucking good. I like it."

We'd been working on it for almost two weeks. Some of my best work, if I'd say so myself.

"Thanks, man." I wrapped his forearm in a sterile bandage. "Make sure you clean it and keep it bandaged."

"Kid, I was getting tattoos while you were still swimming around in your daddy's ball sack," he grumbled. "I think I know what to do."

"Fuck you, man." I chuckled, pulled off the latex gloves and tossed them in the trash bin, then started the cleanup of the room.

"I'll see you bright and early at Church."

"Shit!" I threw the wet paper towels in the trash bin and discarded the used ink. "I forgot about that shit."

According to Reaper, we were having guests courteous of the Mother Chapter, but that was all he would say. I wasn't sure what happened. It was rare King was on guard like he was, and it was even rarer that my brother allowed anyone at the clubhouse, outside of old ladies and club whores.

"Don't be late," Snake warned, pointing at me. "You know how pissed King will be. And I don't want to hear that shit. I'm getting too old for it," he called out over his shoulder as he walked out of the door.

"You don't have to remind me," I mumbled to the empty room. "I've known him my whole fucking life."

King was not only my older brother, he was also the President of Sin City MC's, Oakland chapter. My president. There were three of us. King the oldest, Reaper, the middle son, and me, the youngest–the family screw up. King acted more like my father than my brother. I hated that shit. He was fifteen years older than me, and we had absolutely nothing in common except for the club. For him, it was enough. So, I guess it had to be for me too.

Snake shut the door behind him, and I finished cleaning my workstation. I tattooed away from everyone. I wasn't anti-social, but I couldn't work with the constant chatter of clients and the other artists. I had high-profile clients, too. Sometimes they requested an empty shop, or I ushered them in and out the back door. I kept them separated from our regular clients because crazy fans interrupting daily operations to stalk their favorite celebrity wasn't good for business.

I wiped my hands with paper towels, then tossed them in the bin as I walked out the door towards the waiting area in the front of the shop. Before I made it to the archway separating the main room where the other tattooists worked from the waiting area, the most exquisite, husky, slightly rasped, voice grabbed my attention.

When I reached the waiting area, my heart leaped in my chest when my eyes landed on the most gorgeous woman I'd ever seen in my life. Dark brown locs with golden tips hung at her waist. A long, flower print, off-the-shoulder dress reached the floor, highlighting a curvy figure, and large breasts. Large gold hoop earrings hung from her ears, and gold bangles clanked on her arms as she animatedly talked with another woman and Angel at the receptionist's desk while flipping through a portfolio of my work.

"There he is," Angel called out dramatically, causing me to roll my eyes.

When she faced me, it was like time stopped. Angel and the other woman faded from focus, and all my senses zeroed in on the woman. After gawking for longer than I should have, I shook myself out of my lust-filled stupor. I didn't know who she was, but with every step I took toward her, I knew I was walking toward the woman of my dreams.

"Welcome to Forbidden Ink." I grasped her outstretched hand as I peered down into mesmerizing brown eyes. She was tall despite wearing sandals with no heels but standing at six feet four inches I still had to look down at her. Her grip was firm, her skin as smooth as velvet. "I'm Saint, tattoo artist and owner of Forbidden Ink."

"Hi, I'm Oya. Nice to meet you, Saint."

She released my hand and I wanted so much to grab it again, just to have that tiny connection, feel her skin against mine. Mint and whiskey floated into my nostrils, mixing with the sweet smell of honeysuckle perfume. If sexiness had a smell, it would be hers. A smell that would be imprinted on my soul.

"This is my friend, Raquel."

"Nice to meet you, Oya. Raquel," I said, not removing my eyes from the magnificent woman standing in front of me. "How can I help you, ladies?"

"She wants to get a celebration tattoo," Raquel slurred from behind Oya.

Oya rolled her eyes. "I would like to get a tattoo."

"So, what are we celebrating?" I asked not that it was any of my business.

"Freedom," her friend responded before Oya had the chance to answer.

They both had been drinking. Raquel a little more than Oya.

"Angel, here says you're the best," Oya said.

Her voice was warm and smooth, like honey. I could listen to her all day long. I smiled at the compliment. I was the best, well at least in Oakland. I didn't like to brag. However, I loved when others did it.

"That's what I hear from time to time." She smiled and it was just as captivating as she was. "I'd love to tattoo you, but I'm sorry I can't tattoo you tonight."

Her face fell.

"May I ask why not?" She looked over her shoulder to the neon sign hanging on the window of the shop, blaring open in neon red letters. "The open sign is still on?"

"Yes, we're still open, however, it's the shop's policy not to tattoo anyone who's been drinking."

I motioned to the shop policy sign posted on the wall behind Angel. In large black lettering, it says we will not tattoo anyone if impaired. Although it was posted, Angel should have told her when they entered. But by the smirk on his face, he knew goddamn well what he was doing. They were two stunning women. He wanted to talk to them and keep them in the shop for as long as he could, wasting their time and mine. I had that policy for a reason and wouldn't bend on it. Not even for the woman standing in front of me.

I held my hand up before she could protest. "I take my art and my shop's reputation seriously, Oya. I would never want anyone to regret one of my pieces because they had been drinking."

"That's understandable," she sighed.

"With that being said, I would love to tattoo you, just not tonight. Would you like to do a consultation instead? Then we can schedule an appointment if you want."

"Angel said you're booked for the next two months. I want to get this done as soon as possible before I chicken out."

I was booked for the next two months, but there was no way I'd walk away from having one of my pieces on her smooth, ebony skin. I looked at it as an honor if anyone chose me as their tattoo artist but Oya, she was a work of art.

"You let me worry about that," I said. "I can work you in."

"Are you sure?" she asked, pulling her lip between her teeth.

I resisted the urge to readjust my dick through my jeans. I didn't believe she even realized how sexy she looked. It almost made me envious. I wanted to be the one to bite them.

"I'm positive," I reassured her. "It would be my honor."

"I would like that. Thank you, Saint."

I wasn't a praying man anymore despite the name, yet I prayed one day soon I'd hear her sexy ass voice moaning my name.

Reluctantly, I shifted my focus to Angel. "Close the shop. This will be the last client for tonight. And make sure you're here first thing to open. I've got to go to the clubhouse."

I noticed the look on Oya's face, but I didn't acknowledge it. Everyone in town knew Sin City. And most knew the members were in and out of here. I usually wore my cut, but not tonight. And it wasn't something I elaborated on with clients anyway. If they knew I was a Sinner, they knew. And if they didn't... that didn't concern me.

"You got it, boss," Angel said, doing a mock salute.

"I'll just stay here with Angel," her friend said, giving Angel puppy dog eyes like she'd met her soulmate.

He might give her a good fuck, but Angel was wild as hell and had a lot of growing up to do before he jumped into anything deeper.

I had no problem if Raquel stayed up front. I didn't want Oya distracted if her friend decided to tag along. Consultations were done in private unless the client was totally against it.

"We'll only be a few minutes," I said.

"Take all the time you need," she said while looking between me and Oya, then focusing her attention on Angel.

"Right this way, sweetheart."

Oya nodded and followed me.

"You have a nice place," she said as she followed me through the shop. "It doesn't look like what I thought a tattoo shop would look like."

"Thank you."

I was genuinely happy she took notice. Not too many customers did even though I worked hard on it. Reaper accused me of being too anal because I wanted things to look a certain way. According to him, nobody even cared beyond the tattoo. However, I wanted my clients to have an experience when they walked into my place. Instead of having the typical tattoo shop, I wanted a place clients felt comfortable. Getting a tattoo was nerve-wracking for some people and I wanted to help calm their nerves if possible.

Hardwood floors extend throughout the entire building. Each artist had their workstation separated by a partial wall and a curtain that could be kept open or closed, especially if a specific area was being tattooed. Nobody wanted to see somebody's ass getting inked.

There were six tattoo stations in the main room. Three on each side. At the back wall beside the hallway leading to my office, workstation, employee lounge, and customer restroom, there was a smaller room where all the piercings were done. Track lighting and dark ebony wooden beams accentuated high ceilings. The artwork of the tattoo artists employed at Forbidden Ink covered the pale blue walls, that Reaper gave me hell about. From the walls, floors, lighting, and artwork, all of it tied together the main room of Forbidden Ink. Finally, off to the right, industrial-strength black metal stairs spiraled to a second-floor loft I used if I had late nights and didn't want to drive home.

We made our way down the hallway, passing my private workspace, to my office. I pushed open the office door, allowing Oya to step through, her arm brushing against my chest. She gave an apologetic smile, and I waved it off.

As she passed me, I got a better look at her. To say she was attractive was an understatement. Her presence was beyond anything I'd ever experienced with any woman. The way she walked, the way she talked, and the way she gazed at me just made me want to drown in everything she offered.

"Have a seat," I said, sliding behind my desk and pushing down the urge to bend her over it.

She looked around the room. My office wasn't big, but it had enough space in it where I didn't feel claustrophobic. Small spaces caused me anxiety. It had been that way since I got out of prison. The brick wall facing my glass desk gave it an urban feel, while the white walls and high ceiling gave the illusion of space to the windowless room.

"So, what do you have in mind?"

She pulled her long hair across her shoulder, then sat in the chair in front of my desk with as much elegance I'd ever seen in a woman.

"Before we get started," she said, crossing her long leg over the other, "how long have you been tattooing?"

I loved she asked questions about my experience. Not many of my clients cared because my work usually spoke for itself, but I didn't have a problem answering anything she wanted to know.

I leaned back into my chair, interlacing my fingers behind my head. My black t-shirt tightened across my muscular chest and around my arms. Oya eyed me appreciatively, drifting from my face down my chest before she focused back on my eyes. I did a happy dance on the inside while my face remained stoic. At least the attraction was mutual.

Seven years of my life, I spent locked up in one of the toughest prisons in California, where I learned to tattoo. It was one of the reasons I solely did black-and-white pieces. I started drawing at an early age and even made my own comic when I was younger, but art wasn't something I had a real interest in. My goal since I could remember was to be a priest. That shit seemed hilarious now and a lifetime ago, but I wanted to save my father even though he couldn't be saved. Something as a child I never understood until it finally sunk in after being arrested and convicted for his crime.

Too little too late.

Prison changed my life. I learned my father was a lost cause and learned the ins and outs of how to work on different types and all shades of skin with a prison gun made from a toothbrush, metal string, and an ink pen guided by one of the best artists in the country despite him being an inmate. Randal "Voodoo" Jones, Angel's half-brother, taught me everything I knew about tattooing. Although he'd probably die on the inside, I credit him with everything I knew and my success. I still tried to visit him once a month and keep his account full, so he could get anything he needed. That was all I could do to repay him for changing my life.

I laughed. "Is this your way of asking how old I am?"

"Well, yes." She laughed. "You look so young to have done so much. Your talent and this place are amazing."

She was older. A good fifteen to twenty years older than me if I had to guess. But damn if I didn't want to fuck her. Spread her legs wide, lick and suck her pussy until she came on my tongue and my face was slick with her arousal. At this point, it was all I could think about.

I made a show of looking down at her left hand full of gold and silver rings, except on the finger that mattered. Not to say I wouldn't fuck a married woman. I was an equal-opportunity asshole and fucked just as many married women as single. But with married women came drama. And that was too much to deal with for a piece of ass. Husbands had shown up at my shop and my house. I had too much of a good thing going now to deal with that shit anymore. I had to act like a fucking adult or land my ass back behind bars, which I refused to do.

I flicked my eyes back up to her and licked my lips. "I'm old enough."

The blush staining her skin only made me want her more.

"Do you flirt with all your potential clients?" she asked, smiling.

"Only the ones I want to know more about." I winked, which made her smile widen. "So, what kind of tattoo do you want, Oya?" I asked, trying to get my mind out of the gutter, which seemed impossible where Oya was concerned. I wanted to do nasty shit to her body. "Your name is absolutely beautiful by the way."

"Oh. Thank you. My mother had a thing for African Mythology. Anyway, back to why I'm here," she said laughing. "I'd like, to live is to suffer…"

"To survive is to find some meaning in the suffering," I said, finishing the Fredrich Nietzsche quote.

Her eyes widened. "You know Nietzsche?" she asked, surprise lacing her voice.

"Don't let the tats and good looks fool you, Oya. I'm a man of many talents."

I chuckled at the embarrassment covering her face.

"No, no," she shook her head, "I didn't mean it that way, Saint. I'm sorry. I can't even get my students to like anything concerning Nietzsche. It was just a pleasant surprise."

"Teacher?"

I pulled out my sketch pad from the desk drawer to take notes during our consultation.

"Professor, actually," she said, with unmistakable pride in her voice.

"Ah...smart and good-looking. A deadly combination." Her laugh echoed throughout the room. I couldn't deny it. I wanted to hear more of it. "Okay, gorgeous. Where would you like your tattoo?"

"Somewhere discreet. I don't think my job would like it if it wasn't and I don't want my students asking questions."

Even though her flowing dress covered her figure, I could imagine what she looked like under the billowy fabric. I nodded, taking notes on placement. She was a professional, so I understood her wanting it to be discrete.

"What do you think about your ribs?"

"I'm sure that's painful."

She looked at me horrified.

"I won't lie to you. It's one of the more painful spots. We can do a placement where it can only be seen when you wear a bikini."

"I like that idea, even though I haven't worn a bikini in at least a decade."

"What a shame."

I continued to take notes like I didn't hear her gasp at my comment. I wanted her to know my thoughts without making her uncomfortable or coming across as a pervert.

"Would you like anything else other than the quote?"

I looked up from the sketch pad into chestnut brown eyes swirling with emotion. But she quickly pushed it away and tapped her index finger against her chin.

"I don't think so. I think the words say enough."

I scribbled down my final thoughts on Oya's tattoo, then pulled out my appointment book.

"Let's see. Since I like you, I'm going to make an exception and pencil you in, as I do for my celebrity clients."

I flipped through the pages of the thick notebook. Everyone gave me hell for not going digital with my appointment book and notes, but there was something about writing everything down. Even though I was young, call me old school when it came to that.

"Saint, you don't have to do that."

I loved the way my name sounded on her lips.

"Not a problem." I waved away her protest. "The tattoo isn't complicated. It'll take less than an hour. "

"If you don't think it will interfere with your other clients."

"It won't. Now, I hope you don't mind doing a late night because I'm booked until ten most days."

"No, after ten is fine, only if it's a weekend or on a Tuesday after five."

I browsed my appointment book, looking for the best date and time I could manage. Weekends right now would be out of the question because I would be doing runs for the club for the next few weeks. Or I used that time for my larger pieces.

"How about this Tuesday at ten?" I looked up from my appointment book. "My last appointment should be wrapped up by then."

"Are you sure?" she asked. "Because I can do whatever you need me to do. I know you're busy."

Now if she was any other woman, I'd suggest she could ride my cock, or my face, but there was something about Oya. I wasn't going to be my usual crude self with her.

"I am busy, but you're worth it. I have you down for Tuesday at ten." I pulled out a business card from my desk and scribbled my cell number on the back. "Here's my number. Call me anytime and not just for a tattoo either."

That pretty blush returned to her gorgeous skin, and at that moment I realized Oya was someone I wanted to know more about. She had a deceptive innocence for a woman her age which I loved. But tonight, wasn't the time. I had Church in the morning and Snake was right, King would have my ass if I was late. Not that I wasn't used to him chewing me out for one reason or another, I just hated to have to listen to it.

"Let's get you back to your friend, so she doesn't think I was anything less than a gentleman with you."

She scoffed. "Raquel would cheer you on."

"Is that so?" I asked as we walked back towards the front. "I'll have to remember that the next time I see you. I could use her help."

She looked over her shoulder like she could imagine what I would do to her. Hell, maybe she was imagining all the things she could do to me.

"There you are," Raquel said before she responded, interrupting our moment.

Raquel's mischievous smile widened. She wanted Oya to get laid and I was happy to be the one to do it.

"I just wanted to be thorough," I said, knowing where Raquel's mind was at.

"I'm sure you did." Raquel's eyes moved appreciatively down my body before focusing back on my face. "You should be very thorough. She needs someone to be *extra* focused on her."

Oya groaned. "Raquel."

"What?" Raquel laughed at Oya's embarrassment. "That's one fine ass man and you know just as well as I do you could use a good fuck. I'm sure he could give it to you."

"Oh my god, Raquel!" Oya pushed her friend towards the door. "Sorry, she's drunk."

I leaned against the receptionist's desk. "I don't mind." I winked at her. "I like the way she thinks."

She blushed. "See you Tuesday, Saint."

"Wouldn't miss it, Oya," I called out, as the door closed behind her.

"Interesting two," Angel commented, breaking through my thoughts of how I was going to make my move on Oya.

"Hmmm..."

He laughed, slapping me on the shoulder. "She's so out of your fucking league, my friend," he said as he exited the shop.

She may be out of my league, but that wouldn't stop me. I wanted her. And I always got what I wanted.

I locked the front door behind Angel, cut the lights in the waiting area, then headed to the back. I grabbed the sketch pad and killed the lights in the office. I had Church early in the morning, so there was no point driving across town when the clubhouse was two blocks from the shop.

I plodded up the stairs to the loft, my feet so heavy I could hardly walk. I tossed the sketchpad on the drawing table and flopped on the bed. Thoughts of the sophisticated woman filled my head until sleep found me.

CHAPTER TWO

Church

Everyone except the prospects crammed into the largest room we had at the clubhouse, and we were almost sitting shoulder to shoulder. It wouldn't be long before King would have to expand this place. It wasn't like the club didn't have the money.

I didn't miss the glare from King as I slipped into one of the vacant chairs at the back of the windowless room. I wasn't late, but I wasn't on King time either. I had every intention to be here at a time my brother thought appropriate, so I didn't have to hear him bitch me out, but I didn't get much sleep last night. A certain woman plagued my dreams. I woke up with a hard-on from hell that even jacking off in the shower didn't relieve.

Reaper gave me a what the fuck look and I flipped him off. My middle brother always played peacemaker between King and me and always tried to keep me from catching hell from him. But with King, I could never do anything right no matter how hard I tried.

I eventually grew up and said fuck it. Time in prison will do that to you. Make you realize you can't please everybody. No matter how much I did after being freed, like becoming a successful artist, I couldn't get him to change his mind that I was a screw-up. One crazy night changed how he viewed me. If I could go back and change things, I would. But I can't. I moved on and accepted the decision I made, so why the fuck couldn't he let that shit go.

"I spoke with Grimm, yesterday." King raked his hand through his hair. "That's the reason for this emergency meeting."

If Grimm called, it must be bad. We didn't hear much from the Mother Chapter unless shit was about to hit the fan and it might affect other chapters, or we were doing a large get-together with all the chapters. The look on my brother's face said it wasn't about a get-together.

"He needs us to provide sanctuary and protection to his little sister and her friend," King continued.

"Who are we protecting them from?" Snake asked.

"Bianchi Syndicate," King responded. "The friend is the ex-girlfriend of a Bianchi soldier, who gave intel to the brothers that led to charges against the Bianchi's. According to Grimm, they may have a bounty on their heads."

Of course.

Groans and chatter went around the room. We've had a few run-ins with the Bianchis. They wanted to interfere in our rackets, which included most pro sports teams in California, except for soccer. The Mexican Mafia, the prison gang, controlled that. I'd been on the inside with some of them crazy motherfuckers. Everyone knew not to fuck them. Except the Bianchi's. The Italians were always trying to get a foothold in someone else's business because they didn't like to do the work for themselves.

"Listen. We're not taking a vote on this. They're family," King called out over the noise in the room, and everyone quieted down. "Their fight is our fight, so fucking deal with it. Like I said, these women are our family. We're here to protect them, not fuck them." The men groaned. "Hey!" King called out and the men quieted again. "That's what the club whores are for. So, keep your dicks in your pants and make them feel at home. Church dismissed."

I jumped up and headed for the door with the rest of the brothers. I had an appointment for another back piece, and I hated being late.

"Saint, Reaper, stay behind," King said, stopping me in my tracks.

"Fuck," I mumbled under my breath.

I hoped I could slip out before he could stop me. I made my way to the front of the room where King and Reaper stood while the brothers filed out of the room. I plopped down in the seat in front of them as they leaned against the table at the front of the room.

"Make it quick, I got a client," I said as soon as the door closed, leaving only us three.

"Where have you been?" King asked.

"Where I'm always at, King. Work."

"Da said you haven't been answering his calls."

He crossed his arms over his chest. I admired the tattoo of a lion wearing a crown, I did when I first opened Forbidden Ink. It was a good day. We laughed and talked like family. It was the only time I felt accepted by my older brother.

I shrugged. "Like I said, I've been busy."

"You know how he gets when we don't come around," King said, exasperated like he was tired of having this conversation. He wasn't the only fucking one. I was tired of him trying to fix shit between me and our father. Shit would never be the same between us, and it wasn't up to me to explain why. What happened would stay between us, unless our father took responsibility for the shit, he had done to me. Like I said, I would change shit if I could, but it wasn't on me to change it.

"Not my problem, Prez." He glared at me because I used his title. But that was how he always approached me. Not like a brother, but my leader. What did he expect from me? I sighed. "Look, I have a life and a business to run. I can't be around all the fucking time. If he needs to talk to me, he knows where to find me."

"Drop the attitude, little brother," Reaper said. "We're just checking up on you."

"Fuck you, bro," I said, flipping him off again. "You both know where to find me too."

"Well, it's time you make fucking time for your family, Saint!" King yelled, stopping our bickering before it started. "You have to get over whatever the fuck happened between you and Da because Ma wants to see you."

"Easy for you to say. He didn't fuck you over, King. Or you either, Reaper."

"What do you mean he fucked you over?" King asked, confusion covering his face.

I stood and shoved my hands in my pants. "It doesn't matter. What's done is done."

"If you don't tell us what the hell you're talking about, how do you expect us to understand, Gavin?" Reaper asked. "How do you expect us to help fix it?

"I don't expect either one of you to fix shit!"

That was what they both don't understand. I don't expect anyone to fix anything. Those seven years were gone. Whether my father owned up to anything still didn't change shit.

I dropped my head and focused on my breathing, trying to calm my anger. "Look, I'll try to make time to go see Ma, but I can't promise anything. I'm booked solid," I said, ignoring Reaper's questions.

If they wanted answers, I wasn't the person to ask. Our da was the person they needed to talk to. My brothers wanted me to be the bad guy so bad, never stopping to think I wasn't the problem.

I turned on my heels and made my way to the door. "Do more than try, Saint. I'm not fucking asking you to, I'm telling you to," King ordered. "And your ass better be here tonight."

I slammed the door, not responding to him. What the hell did he think he could do to me? I was a grown-ass man who only listened to him if it had to do with the club. My relationship with our parents didn't have shit to do with the club. If my father and me stayed estranged that was my fucking business, no one else's. There was more to the fucking story than they knew. So no, I'd never forgive him for the shit he had done and the years of my life it cost.

I made my way down the porch of the clubhouse bypassing the club whores, a few of the brothers, and prospects as they prepared for the bonfire tonight. Not the place I wanted to be, but I was a Sinner until the day I died. So, I'd stop by tonight, show my face for a few hours, and then skip out.

CHAPTER THREE

Forbidden Ink

I eyed the clock on the wall. I'd been booked solid and was tired as fuck. But it was only nine thirty and I couldn't wait to see Oya again. To say she plagued my mind the past few days would be an understatement. Her smell, her laugh, and the way she looked at me like she wanted to tear my clothes off as much as I wanted to tear hers off played over in my mind. And despite the hectic few days since I saw her that first night, it was like the days had flown by.

I went to the bonfire like King demanded, but only stayed a few hours. It was all I could manage because regardless of what was going on at the club, I still had a business to run. I drank way too much, smoked even more, and enjoyed a night of relaxation. I hated to admit it, but I needed the break. I hadn't had a real vacation in a long time. Not that I couldn't afford one, I hated leaving my business in the hands of other people. I could admit, I was a control freak, especially when it came to what was mine.

At the bonfire, I met the two women Grimm sent, and it looked like King had finally met his match with Alana Robinson. The best friend of Grimm's sister. She gave him hell, and I loved every minute of it. It wasn't often my brother was left speechless and I thoroughly enjoyed watching him have his balls handed to him by the feisty woman. She didn't care he was president. She didn't care that everyone around him asked how high when he said fucking jump. She treated him like an ordinary person, not the badass leader of a one-percenter club. Something he wasn't used to. But with Alana around until everything was cleared up with the Bianchis, he'd have to get used to it because I didn't see her pulling any punches. He would either kill her or fall head over heels in love with her. It was still a toss-up.

I paused setting up my work area when there was a light knock on the door. "Come in."

The door slowly opened, and Oya peeked her head in. When she saw me, her eyes brightened, and my fucking heart stopped in my chest. If she'd looked at me like that until the day I died, I'd die a happy man. I pushed the feeling down, so I didn't come across like a creep, walked over to the door, and ushered her in, closing it behind me.

"Angel, just told me to head on back," she said with her hands, and a clutch in front of her body as she looked around the room, "I hope that's fine?"

Today she had on a white silk blouse, a bright pink skirt that stopped just above the knee, which looked like it was in love with her body with how it hugged her curves, and white strappy heels that added at least three inches to her height. Just looking at her made me wonder how much of a chance I had with a woman like her. She was educated, and classy. I was an ex-con covered in ink, not to mention at least ten years younger than her, if not more. Angel was right. She was completely out of my fucking league, but I was a glutton for punishment.

"Of course. He should be locking up the front and heading out. So, it's just you and me. Hope that's cool with you?"

"Yeah, sure," she said. "So, this is where you do your thing, huh?"

"It is. I work with celebrities, so I have to be separated from the crowd." She faced me, and nervous energy rolled off her in waves. I grasped her hands. "There's no need to be nervous. I'll take care of you. You ready?"

She took in a deep breath and exhaled, then nodded. "I'm ready."

I winked, then faced away from her. "Take your shirt off."

I pulled out a pair of packaged gloves from the drawer where I kept all my supplies, including needles. I'd already set up the ink and stenciled the quote. All I had left to do was prep her skin. I faced her. Her eyes widened, and she still had her shirt on.

"Oya?"

"I'm so...sorry," she said, fumbling over her words. "What did you say?"

I took a step towards her. "I said, take off your shirt." I tilted my head at the look of horror on her face. I grabbed her shoulders and moved my hands up and down the silk covering her arms. "Babe, I can't do a tattoo on your ribs unless you take your shirt off."

"I know it's just..."

I stood in her space, but she didn't seem bothered by the closeness, and neither was I.

"Now tell me what's the problem."

She hid behind her hands, covering her face. "It's so embarrassing," she groaned.

I pulled her hands from her face and grasped them. "I've got time."

"You remember the celebration Raquel mentioned when we first came into the shop?" she asked, looking into my eyes.

"I remember you avoiding what she said."

"You remember that, huh?" she asked, laughing. "Anyway, we were celebrating my divorce."

"So, congratulations are in order?" I asked with a chuckle, but I was interested if she was torn up over it. I wasn't into capitalizing on her heartbreak. But if there was a chance I could have her under me, I would take it.

"Yes, congratulations are definitely in order. It had been a long time coming. Oh my god, I can't believe I'm going to tell you this."

"You'd be amazed the stories and deep dark secrets I hear from my clients. Some treat me like their therapist or their priest." I laughed, but I was serious. I'd been told so much shit over the years, especially when I was in prison, tattooing inmates. "But I don't want to pressure you. I just want you to have the best experience."

"You're so sweet."

"Well, that's not a word, I'm used to a woman calling me, but from you, I'll take it." I winked. "So, what's got you so shy?"

She took a deep breath and released it. "I froze because no other man has seen me without my clothing since my ex-husband. And as you can see, I'm not young anymore. Things aren't how they used to be."

"You're beyond gorgeous, Oya, regardless of your age. And if I'm being honest, I want to see you. But if it makes you uncomfortable, I'll shut my eyes and turn my back. Whatever you need me to do."

"You want to see me?" she asked surprised.

"Who the fuck wouldn't?" I asked standing in front of her. I turned her towards the mirror hanging on the wall as I stood behind her with my hands resting on her shoulders. "This hair." I twirled a loc around my finger. "Your skin." I ran my finger down her jawline. "You are the most attractive woman, I've ever seen."

She stared at me in the mirror like she couldn't believe the words coming out of my mouth. It was the truth. Oya was a woman who stood out above everyone else. She was indescribable. She was fucking chef's kiss exquisite.

"Thank you, Saint."

I shrugged. "I'm only speaking the truth."

She kept her eyes trained on me as she slowly started to unbutton the silk blouse she wore after taking a deep breath and letting my words sink in. My cock hardened. There was no fucking way she couldn't feel me against her ass, but she kept her eyes trained on me. Fuck, I was salivating just waiting, watching this woman undress for me.

If not for me, I could pretend it was just for me.

It was normal for people to undress in front of me. People get tattoos anywhere there was skin. I'd tattooed tits, asses, dicks, and cunts. You name it, I'd done it. So, I was used to naked people. But Oya...Oya wasn't even going to be completely nude. Just her removing her shirt was enough to have me panting.

I grabbed the silk blouse from her hand as she stood in front of the mirror in a black lace bra, covering ample-sized breasts, specks of dark skin peeking through. She looked like a fucking goddess. I hung the shirt on the rack in the corner customers used for their clothes if they needed to undress.

I felt her eyes track me throughout the room. The hum vibrating through my body was exciting and unnerving. I've never wanted to experience a woman as much as I wanted to experience the walls of

Oya's pussy fluttering around my cock, or her pussy juices on my tongue so bad. I paused for a moment and pushed down my desires. This wasn't about me getting my dick wet, I reminded myself. She wanted a tattoo, nothing more.

I prepared the gun, then finally looked at her again. She still stood in front of the mirror, gazing at me through the reflection. "What's on your mind?" she asked.

"Do you really want to know?" I asked, taking a step closer to her.

She faced me. I knew she wanted me. It showed brightly in her eyes. But she would have to take the first step because if I had Oya once, it wouldn't be just one time. She was just that kind of woman.

"I do," she answered.

I walked forward until I stood in front of her. Her chest rose quickly, expecting my answer.

"I was just thinking how much I would love for you to come in my mouth." I licked my lips just thinking about the moisture touching my tongue. Her tiny gasp urged me further. "How good it will feel to have your cunt wrapped tightly around my cock."

Her brown eyes darkened.

"Would you like that, sweetheart?" I asked.

Taking a leap of faith, I brushed the pads of my thumbs over her rigid nipples, still encased in her lace bra. Her eyes closed on contact. It was probably forward of me, but I couldn't help it. I loved seeing her reaction.

"Would you like my tongue and cock buried deep in your wet pussy?"

"Saint," she moaned, arching towards me.

"All you have to do is ask, Oya." I grasped both her breasts, squeezing them in my hands, loving how heavy they were, how soft. I could just imagine them in my mouth. "Tell me, and I'll give you the fucking world."

"But you don't know me."

"I don't." I ran my tongue up the column of her neck, relishing in the taste of her skin. "But I want to. All you have to do is say the word."

Her eyes focused on me, heavy with lust. "I want it."

I smirked. "Want what, Oya?"

"I want you, Saint." She unhooked her bra, the fabric falling to the floor. "I want you inside of me."

There was the confident woman I first met. Bashful Oya was cute, but this woman had fire simmering in her body, and I wanted to be doused in her flames.

"Strip."

I took a step away from her, giving her space to finish undressing and giving me time to calm down before I fucked her against the mirror. She removed her skirt and underwear. I took her black lacy thong and sniffed it, then shoved the fabric in my pocket. "These are mine, now. For when I can't have you."

She stood before me, bare. It was the most glorious sight, I'd ever seen. "You are fucking amazing." I squeezed both of her tits, and she groaned. "So, fucking responsive. In the chair," I ordered.

She slid into the tattoo chair without hesitation, and I pulled the rolling stool in front of her and sat. I pushed her legs apart, getting a view of the prettiest cunt I'd ever seen. Chocolate, moist petals hiding a pink center. Dripping and plump. Ripe and ready for my tongue and my dick.

Soft and wet, I ran my index finger through her slit, parting her folds. Then I licked from the bottom to the top of her pussy, swirling my pierced tongue around her clit. I groaned as her taste covered my tongue and her scent filled my nostrils. Gripping her thighs, I pulled her closer, nipping, then flicking her clit until she started squirming from my touch. She gripped my head pulling me closer to her body.

"I could fucking eat your pussy until the day I die, Oya."

I gazed up at her through lust-filled eyes, while I continued to devour her. I sucked her clit in my mouth, alternating between sucking gently and harder. A gush of wetness flooded my mouth, and my eyes rolled. If her pussy tasted this good, I could only imagine how she would feel while I fucked her.

I inserted two fingers inside her, moving them in and out of her slowly. Her hips met the thrust of my fingers. Her walls fluttered, and it was crazy how wet she became. As I fucked her with my fingers and tongue, her moans and scent filled the room.

"Damn," she moaned, her hips slightly lifting from the chair, "that feels so good."

Never had I fucked a woman at work. Not that any hadn't offered, I just tried to keep pleasure separated from my business. But there wasn't any way I'd say no to Oya. I wanted her screaming my name and I couldn't wait for a more appropriate place. And every time I stepped into this room, the memory of this would always be on my mind.

I sucked her clit until she rocked her hips against my tongue. My fingers picked up the pace, and her channel tightened around them as I brought her closer to the edge. I wanted to see her come. I wanted to see her face blanketed in the pleasure only I could give her.

My eyes lifted to hers. I expected hers to be closed, but they weren't. She gazed at me while she worked her hips against my tongue and fingers. I couldn't wait to be inside her. I sucked harder on her clit, then shoved another finger inside her, causing her to explode with my name on her lips.

"Fuck you are so stunning when you come," I said, moving my fingers in and out of her until she came down from her orgasm.

I stood and pushed the stool away. My dick pressed mercilessly against my jeans. I rubbed my erection through the thick fabric. Her eyes drifted down to my crotch and lust gazed over her eyes again.

"Are you ready for my cock?"

"Yes," she said without any hesitation.

I unbuttoned, then unzipped my jeans, and pushed them down below my knees along with my boxer briefs. I grasped my pierced shaft and ran my hand from the tip to the base a few times. Her eyes widened and I chuckled.

"You want to put that inside me?" she asked, pointing at my dick. "Saint, you can't be serious?"

I laughed. I couldn't control it. She hadn't been the only woman surprised or scared when they saw the silver barbels along the bottom of my shaft that ran from the base to the head. Every woman questioned once they saw my Jacob's Ladder if it would hurt. Would I fit? But I always assured them when they got a taste of my dick, there was no going back.

"Trust me. You'll be begging me to fuck you." I winked and she looked down at my dick, then back at me skeptically. I held down my laughter. "Stand, and bend over, Oya. I can show you better than I can tell you."

She looked down at my shaft leaking precum from the red mushroomed tip again but complied.

"I'm not going to be gentle." I ran my finger down her spine, then through the crack of her ass, and her wet pussy, causing her to shiver. "I'm going to fuck you until you beg me to fill you with my cum."

Without any warning, I thrust into her to the hilt, and I was in fucking heaven. Pure bliss encompassed me. If I didn't know before, I knew it now. Oya was mine. Fuck any other woman. I was home. I gripped her wide hips, pulled her hard, and flush against my pelvis. She gripped the chair, her nails digging into the black leather.

"Oh!" she screamed. "Oh fuck!"

"Fuck you feel good." I wasn't going to last long but I didn't give a fuck. This wouldn't be the last time I fucked her, even though she didn't know it yet. "Damn, Oya, this pussy is mine."

My fingers dug into the flesh of her hips as I pulled her harder and faster, back, and forth along my cock. Grunts, moans, and the sounds of flesh against flesh echoed throughout the room and it was like music to my damn ears. Music, I didn't want to stop but I didn't have a choice. My bars were hitting her spot. Her pussy was getting wetter and clenching me.

I slapped her ass, a gorgeous red spot forming on her ebony skin. "Saint!" she screamed as her cunt clamped down on my length like a vice. And that was all it took. I sped up my thrusts, relishing in the warmth, the wetness of what I knew would ruin me for any other woman. Fuck her age. Shit, fuck mine. Oya was going to be mine until I left this miserable fucking earth.

"This pussy is mine until I die, Oya."

Such a crazy statement to make, but I was damn serious. No one else's dick would get this pleasure if I had anything to say about it. I slammed into her harder, over, and over again, watching her ass bounce from each push into her. I chased the familiar tingle starting at my toes as it quickly covered my entire body. Quicker than I wanted. But we had all night. At least I hoped we had all night.

"Please, Saint," she begged.

Her pleas for pleasure slowed me down, so I could hit that magical spot again. I moved in tandem with her as she met my thrusts. Her screams got louder, echoing my grunts. "Fuck, sweetheart," I groaned as my orgasm washed over me like a warm tidal wave of euphoria.

I was high as a motherfucker from ecstasy. Warm ropes of cum filled her as I relished in sweet fucking bliss only her pussy provided. I pumped in and out of her until her greedy cunt took everything I had as she fell over in bliss with me.

Finally, when we both came down, I pulled out, kneeled behind her, then spread her folds. My cum and hers leaked from inside her and it was the most erotic thing I'd ever seen. I stuck my tongue inside her, tasting our salty, musky mixture.

"Fucking manna from heaven," I mumbled against her skin.

I was a nasty motherfucker, and I couldn't wait until I dirtied her too. It was irrational how much I wanted this woman, but I did. It was irrational licking her and my cum from her body but I did it anyway. Whatever brought her pleasure, whatever made her scream my name I would do it.

I licked, flicked, and sucked until she leaked more of my cum, hers, and more arousal. I pulled her folds further apart, tonguing her, watching her pink skin become wetter. "Saint, I'm coming!" she screamed as her hips furiously rode my mouth.

Once again, I hated for it to end, but I wanted her trembling at my touch.

"Come, sweetheart. Come all over my face."

"Oh!" she yelled, her juices squirting all over my face, dripping down my chin. Her body trembled while I drank from her like a thirsty man.

She slumped on the chair. I stood and gripped my shaft which had already started to harden again. I ran my hand up and down my sensitive piercings. I wanted so bad to be inside her again, but I'd give her a brief moment to recover.

She turned over and sat in the chair, gazing at me wide-eyed like she couldn't believe I was still hard. I let go of my shaft and propped her legs on the arms of the chair. She was wide open for me. I got an eye full of her body, while she hungrily eyed my cock.

Her shaved pussy glistened under the fluorescent lighting. Her large breasts weren't perky like most women I'd been with. Her stomach wasn't flat, and the skin was covered with faint stretchmarks, and all of it only added to her beauty. All of it made me want to fuck her more. Fuck her harder.

I gripped my dick tighter. It was hard as steel, a bead of precum shining at the tip. "You are so fucking beautiful." I squeezed my cock, my eyes briefly closing from the sensation moving through me. "Do you see what you do to me? Touch your tits, Oya," I said, my command laced with nothing but desire for the sexiest woman lying in front of me with her pussy there for the taking.

Her hands moved to her breasts, then she tweaked, and twisted her taut nipples between her fingers. I groaned, moving my hand up and down my shaft, a shiver passing over me each time my hand grazed my piercings.

"Touch my pussy," I commanded.

"Your pussy?" she asked, with a small smirk as she slowly moved her hand down her stomach, until she reached her center.

"Yeah, sweetheart." I moved my hand faster as I watched her play in her pretty pussy. "Mine."

Damn, I didn't think she could get any sexier, but watching her touch herself was some erotic shit I'd never experienced.

"Make yourself come, babe. I want to see how your pussy clenches around your fingers."

My voice was raspy, low, and so full of want I barely recognized the sound as my own. She had me sounding like a possessed man.

She dipped two fingers in her channel, then brought them to her clit. Her eyes closed.

I jacked off harder, faster watching her face morph into pure bliss. "Open your eyes, Oya," I ordered. "I want you to see what you do to me."

Her eyes opened, and her tongue darting across her lips had me wishing it was the head of my cock.

"Fuck I'm close," I admitted stepping closer to her. I wanted to make sure I covered her magnificent body. "Can I come on you baby?"

"Yes," she moaned as she rode her fingers. "Come on me."

I stroked my length faster passing my hand over the pierced head of my cock. That was all it took to send me over the edge. My body tingled and shuddered as my orgasm barreled through me. "Fuck Oya," I hissed.

Cum landed on her tits, stomach, and her bare glistening pussy. I continued to stroke myself until there was nothing left. While getting my breaths under control I watched in pure fucking delight as she ran her finger through my cum, then licked it off her finger. She groaned like it was the most glorious thing she'd ever tasted.

"Are you fucking trying to kill me?" I asked as she dropped her legs from the armrests of the chair, laughing.

"You started this, Saint, not me."

I took a few paper towels and handed them to her so she could clean my seed from her skin, then I took a handful, and cleaned my cock, shuddering from the sensitivity. She handed me the soiled paper towels and I tossed them in the trash, then reached for her outstretched hand, helping her from the chair.

I pulled her to my frame and gazed into her eyes. "What?" she whispered.

"I don't know." I squeezed her a little tighter, her breasts touching my chest. "I'm feeling all kinds of shit."

A smile blanketed her face as she hooked her arms around her neck. "Me too, but you know this can't happen, right?"

My heart slammed against my chest. "You ever had a moment where shit just aligned, and you felt nothing but peace?"

She nodded.

"This is what happened the first night I met you."

I closed my eyes and took in a couple of deep breaths, to calm myself, then opened them. She waited patiently while I got my thoughts together, and I was grateful. I wanted to be upfront. I wanted something with her, even though I wasn't sure what I exactly wanted.

"I haven't had it easy, Oya," I said, and her eyes saddened, but I wasn't looking for her pity. "No. No. Don't do that."

"Don't do what?" she asked.

"Pity me. I made a choice and I live with it every day."

"Okay," she replied.

"Anyway, what you see took a lot of time and hard work. But before I got to this point, I'd hit my lowest. Even though I love what

I do, something has always been missing, then you came in and it was like maybe things could be different for me."

"Saint..."

"Gavin," I said, interrupting her statement.

Not only did I not want to hear what she had to say, but I also wanted her to know my real name. The only people who called me Gavin were my brothers, sometimes, and my mother who I hadn't talked to in months. Every woman I'd been with since I'd gotten out of prison, my brothers, and even my clients all called me Saint.

"Excuse me?" she asked, her brows knitted in confusion.

"Gavin Lawson. My name is Gavin, not Saint."

She smiled. "Gavin. I'm not denying there's something about you." She sighed. "What we just shared was amazing."

"I hear a but coming," I said, stepping away from her.

Her shoulders slumped, but I ignored it. I pulled up my pants and handed her clothes to her. She grabbed them, but sadness covered her face.

I knew where the conversation was headed, and I hated it. Of course, I didn't expect us to magically start a relationship. I wasn't idiotic. But I wanted to spend more time with her to see if something could develop between us. If not a relationship, maybe a friendship.

Who the fuck was I kidding? Angel was right. She was out of my league.

"We don't know each other."

"But we could get to know one another," I replied as I watched her dress. I wanted so badly to snatch the fabric back off her body.

"Gavin. I just divorced my husband of twenty-two years."

"And what does that have to do with me, Oya? I just want to get to know you. What's so wrong with that?"

She laughed. "How old are you, Gavin?"

"What's my age have to do with anything?" I asked a little defensively.

Yes, I was younger than her, but that shit didn't matter to me. I saw a woman I wanted to know more about. Fuck her age and mine.

"A lot." She sighed. "A lot of men don't understand that it may be acceptable for them to date a younger woman, but it doesn't work the same for women. I'm forty-six years old, Gavin. I also have a son who's probably a few years younger than you."

She didn't look her age, and I was shocked she even had a son. None of it changed my mind about what I thought of her. I still wanted her, but I could see where she was coming from. She had a son my age. How would I deal with that? Which was probably the reason she told me. But I also had things she didn't know about me too. Like I'd been convicted and sent to prison when I was seventeen years old and had only been out for three years. Could she handle that?

After a few moments of silence, she smiled but it didn't quite reach her eyes. "I've got to go. I've got work in the morning."

I reached for her hand. "Please stay," I said, my heart squeezing in my chest.

If she walked out tonight, this was possibly the last time I'd see her. And I didn't want that. I didn't know shit about Oya. But I didn't want that to stop whatever this could be. I could learn about her, and she could learn about me.

"I can't," she said, and my shoulders deflated.

She intertwined our fingers and walked towards the door. I didn't fight her. She'd made up her mind. Maybe in a few days, she might think differently, and I still had to do her tattoo. When we reached the front of the shop, she faced me.

"I still owe you a tattoo."

She laughed and it was like music to my ears. "I'll reschedule. I promise." She kissed me on the lips, then pulled away. "You'll never understand how much this night meant to me. Thank you, Gavin."

She pushed open the door and walked to her car parked in front of the shop. She unlocked the doors, and glanced up at me, giving me a small wave before she slid behind the wheel and pulled away from the curb.

Tonight, hadn't gone as I expected although it was one of the most erotic and intense experiences of my life. I understood Oya's position, but I wouldn't give up that easily. It might be out of the ordinary for someone my age to be interested in an older woman, but there was just something special about her. I didn't think I could walk away without knowing for sure if there could be something special between us.

I locked up, and trudged up the stairs to the loft, to get ready for tomorrow. I had a full day, but I'd also work on trying to get Oya to at least give me a chance.

CHAPTER FOUR

Clubhouse

With my elbows planted on the worn wooden bar at the clubhouse, I took a swig from my fourth bottle of beer. We patched in two of the Prospects and we were celebrating. All the brothers were here, and the clubhouse was packed with women willing to do anything to get a brother's attention. I didn't know how many times I turned down sex and blowjobs, tonight. A few weeks ago, I'd gladly taken someone up on their offer but not now.

Cigarette and weed smoke mingled with the scent of sex, saturating the air. Loud music thumped through the surround sound as the celebration of adding two more Sinners to the fold ratcheted up. Tonight, was a rare one for me. I had a day off and I wanted to drown away my sorrows. It had been three weeks since I'd seen or talked to Oya. I hadn't been able to find out anything about her.

"Why the hell do you look like you lost your best friend?" Reaper asked as he slid on the stool beside me, then picked up the bottle of beer the Prospect sat in front of him. "Hope it doesn't have anything to do with Raven," he grumbled, "Smoke said she had been asking the whores about you. Fucking cunt," he sneered.

Raven Moriarty used to be one of the club whores I'd taken an interest in. Stupid, I know, but when I got out of prison, I was high on freedom, and she was willing. Her attention turned into something it shouldn't have. She'd gotten clingy, wanting me to brand her, and call her my old lady. Reaper and even King warned me that was all she wanted like most of the women who hung around the clubhouse. But I didn't listen. I was enjoying myself. She wasn't my old lady, and I didn't want one.

Then one day Raven claimed she was pregnant with my kid. Suck it up Saint and deal with your shit, I told myself. And for seven months I took care of her. Got her anything the baby or she said she needed. Even put her ass up in an apartment across town, not too far from my home, so she'd have a nice place to stay once the baby came. I wasn't treating her like my old lady, but I was treating her like the mother of my kid. Or so I thought. The day she went into labor, I wasn't the only person at the hospital claiming to be the father. Needless to say, I dodged a bullet despite all the cash I wasted to take care of a kid that wasn't even mine and a bitch that knew it.

"Fuck you, bro." I took another swig. "Trust me, I learned my fucking lesson with that one. Just got shit on my mind."

"Want to talk about it?" He spun the stool towards me. The older he got the more he looked like our mother. King and me on the other hand had been cursed with our *Da's* looks. "Gav, you know you can talk to me, man. I can see something's bothering you."

Anytime Reaper wanted to connect with me on a blood brother level and not like a club brother he always called me Gav. It was when I knew he wanted me to talk to him about what was happening in my life.

"I met someone."

"Okay." He shrugged. "So, why is that such a bad thing?"

"She's older. Doesn't believe anything can develop between us."

"Wait." He leaned forward like he was about to hear a deep dark secret. "How much older?"

There was a time I told Reaper everything. We were close before I went to prison and were steadily getting back like we were. I'd changed in the time I was away and so had he. It was taking time, but at least we were trying to be like we were.

"She's older than King."

"Shut the fuck up!" His smile widened. "A cougar. I bet she chewed your ass up and spit you out, didn't she? Older bitches got that good shit, bro. Seriously. They know what the hell they're doing," he said with a faraway look in his eyes.

"So, you know what I'm talking about?"

"Shit yeah, man. I've had some wild times with a few older women. She's got you twisted, don't she?"

He laughed and I punched him in the shoulder. "Man," I sighed, "that was the best experience of my fucking life. There's just something about her."

"Then what's the problem?" Reaper asked then took another sip of his beer. "If you're into her and she's into you, why not see where it goes?"

"I want to, but she just got divorced. The age gap's an issue for her and she's got a kid a few years younger than me."

He whistled. "Now the kid could be a problem."

That was the reason I froze. Despite the age difference, the kid may be a hurdle I can't jump. And I wouldn't expect any woman to choose me over their child despite how much I wanted her.

"That's the thing, I think I'm willing to deal with it just to get to know more about her."

"And that's the problem right there, bro."

He pointed to me, and my brows knitted together. I was confused. I thought I could deal with her having a kid my age. Although I was an ex-con, I'd made something of my life. I owned my own business, my own house, car, and motorcycle. For someone who lost everything, I thought I was doing good for myself. I was in a position to have someone like Oya in my life.

"What?" I asked.

"You can't think, Gavin. You have to know you're willing to deal with her having a grown-ass kid. I'm sure this woman has her shit together, am I right?"

"She does."

"Well, she's not going to cause strife in her life just because you *think* you can deal with things." He shook his head and sighed. "You're not dealing with someone your age. Shit, you're not dealing with someone my age. This woman has life experience. Experience you could only dream of. She knows what she wants out of life, out of a relationship whether intimate or friendly. For you to have a chance with someone like that your ass better know too."

"Well, how does she know that I'm not ready?"

"She knows because she left your ass standing there." He gulped down the rest of his beer and turned back towards the crowd. "If she's what you want, you have to prove that shit to her."

The buzzing of my cell phone in my pocket stopped my reply. I pulled out my phone from my back pocket and read the text. Shock, then fucking relief hit my system.

"That her?" Reaper asked, leaning over, trying to read the message from Oya.

"Yeah, she wants to meet up, tonight," I responded while typing out my reply. Once done, I stood and slid my phone back into my pocket.

Lila, one of the club's whores, slid between Reaper's legs as he took a swig of beer, smiling as she whispered something in his ear.

"You good enough to ride?" he asked, palming her ass while she kissed his neck.

"Of course." I headed toward the door. "See you later," I called out over my shoulder.

I couldn't help the relief and joy moving through me. I thought I'd never hear from her. And tonight, I'd show her I was worth a chance.

· · · • • · • · · ·

Embers

In less than twenty minutes I pulled into the parking lot of Embers, one of Oakland's newer bar and grills. The music and laughter from the outside patio off to the left of the building filtered into the parking lot across the street. I didn't miss the stares from the patrons in the parking lot. Or how the women clutched their purses closer to them and how their men wrapped their arms tighter around their girlfriends and wives. I also didn't miss the whispers. I'd gotten used to it especially now that I was covered in tattoos and a patched member of Sin City MC.

I ignored the gawkers as I jogged across the two-lane side street in front of Embers. The security stationed at the entrance, no doubt either former military or off-duty police officers, eyed me warily as I entered the bar, proudly wearing my cut.

Oakland was our territory. No other mc would dare step foot here. Everyone knew the Sinners and it was something I needed to discuss with Oya. I was a Sinner for life. I wanted her, but my club wasn't up for debate much like her having a kid wasn't. My club and her kid were permanently a part of our lives no matter who else was in it.

Pushing my way through the small crowd gathered around a table of women throwing back shots in barely there clothing not too far from the entrance, I scanned the bar. It had been three weeks since I'd seen her, and I couldn't lie, I craved her. Her smell. Her smile. Her taste. I craved it all. She might have thought the words spoken to her while we fucked were just words of passion, but I was dead ass serious. She was mine now, I just had to prove it to her.

I never chased women. For the seven years, I was locked up, King worked it out where I had a woman whenever I needed one and when I got out, it was no different. They were always around. I could choose who I wanted and how many I wanted.

Wanting Oya was something new for me and I was willing to do all the chasing no matter how long she ran.

On the ride here, I had time to think. How do I approach a woman like her? I rarely took advice from Reaper. He wasn't exactly the poster boy for relationships, but I did believe he was right. Oya had her shit together. She wouldn't be looking for something or someone who did things half-assed.

I spotted her on the other side of the circular bar sitting at the center of the room, and I stopped in my tracks. She repeatedly dipped an olive in and out of a martini. Nervousness was something I'd never felt around women, but it was different with her. Everything was different with her. She contacted me. Was she finally ready to see if this was something she wanted to pursue?

The sound of some rock song, pool balls clapping against each other, patrons laughing and talking with one another filtered through the dimly lit room. I thought Oya looked out of place because she was so elegant. Not saying Embers was a dive bar, but it wasn't a scene I pictured Oya frequenting. It was too uppity for someone like me, but not classy enough for someone like her.

Making my way to her, I didn't miss the lustful eyes of some of the women I passed, the men who glared, mad that their old ladies lusted after the bad boy, and others who recognized the Sinners' patches. When she spotted me, a smile that could make a man drop dead crossed her face and I couldn't stop the one lifting at the corners of my mouth. It was like a weight on my chest lifted and peace settled over me like the first day I met her.

"Hi," she said when I reached her side.

I leaned down and kissed her cheek. Loving the feel of her soft skin against my lips. "Hi," I replied, pulling out the bar chair beside her, then sitting. "Long time, no see."

"I know. I'm sorry I just disappeared on you." She took a deep breath and released it. "I've been going through some stuff with my ex-husband."

I stiffened. I didn't like the sound of her voice or the look of anger in her eyes.

"What?" I asked needing her to tell me what was going on when in fact I didn't have the right to know anything about her life.

"He's just having a hard time coming to terms with me moving on with my life." She shrugged like it was nothing, but I wasn't so sure. I'd witnessed bitter men do horrible things just for the hell of it. Her nonchalant attitude didn't assuage my concern or anger.

"He's giving you shit?" I asked, trying to hide my anger.

She hadn't asked for my help, but I would if she needed it.

"It's nothing you need to worry about. I can manage Thomas." She took a sip of her martini. "Would you like something to drink?" she asked, waving the bartender over and changing the subject.

I probably shouldn't since I already had four beers, but I needed to calm down. I could always get one of the prospects to come get me if I couldn't drive.

The bartender made her way to us with a predatory glint in her eyes. Long auburn hair, big tits, a small waist, and decently wide hips, she would be someone I'd take home in a heartbeat. But that was before I met Oya. None of that appealed to me now. Not saying the woman wasn't nice to look at, she just wasn't the woman who had my attention.

"What can I get you, sweetheart?" she asked me, planting her forearms on the bar top, giving me the perfect view of her ample cleavage.

I smirked, wrapping my arms around Oya's shoulder ignoring her attempt to flirt. "What would you like, baby?" She laid her head against me playing along, and the bartender quickly rose from the bar top. "Another Vodka Martini neat, sweetheart?"

I kissed her on the head, then focused back on the bartender. The lust still danced in her eyes but this time it was mixed with envy. "Vodka Martini neat for my woman, and a pint of Guinness for me."

She nodded and quickly walked away. Oya lifted her head, then gazed at me. We both started laughing uncontrollably. We calmed down when the bartender sat both our drinks in front of us, barely giving us a second look.

"Did you see her face?" Oya asked, then took a sip of her drink.

"I did." I took a sip of my beer, then sat it on the bar top. "She looked like she could eat shit."

We both paused for a moment then started laughing again. It was amazing how easy it was with her. I wasn't shy, but when I had female clients, the conversations were mostly one-sided. I wasn't a big flirt, but women openly flirted with me all the time. I never initiated.

"How often does that happen?" she asked, humor lacing her voice.

"Probably not as much as it happens to you," I responded, laughing.

She arched her brow, then I knew she wanted me to answer. Not sure why she'd want to know. "It happens more often than I like to admit."

"Hmm..."

"Hmm?" I repeated with a smirk. "What does that mean?"

"Just imagining all the women you've had in that same room we..."

"Hold on," I say, interrupting her comment. "What we shared, I've never done that before with any woman in that room or any place else. I'm not claiming to be an angel, Oya, however the time we shared was special to me even if it wasn't to you."

"It was special to me, too," she murmured. "You made me feel like the most beautiful woman in the world. But you froze when I told you about my son."

"Not for the reason you think." I gulped down the last of my beer. "I want you, Oya. We can have something special. I have no doubt it will be a struggle for him but not for me."

"He will struggle," she said. "He's very protective because my relationship with his father wasn't the best." She gazed at me and like before, it was like she stared into my soul. There had to be more to us. This woman was the one meant for me despite the age difference. I knew it. I felt it. "He'd also want me to be happy."

"You think I can make you happy?"

My heart pounded against my chest. This was it. We needed to talk more about our lives, and who we were but there was a chance.

"I can hope, Gavin. You're so young." She sighed. "You have so much life to live. So much life ahead of you to experience. Why in the hell do you want a forty-something-year-old divorced woman, with a kid your age."

"Because I'm drawn to you, Oya." I grasped her hands. "I don't know why but I want to get to know you."

"If my son was thinking about doing something like this, I'd try to talk him out of it," she confessed. "I'd question why a woman my age would want someone so young."

"Good thing this is us then," I said, smiling.

"Yeah, it is. Do you want to go someplace a little quieter? I can tell you whatever you want to know about me, and you can tell me how you became a Sinner?"

I arched my brow and she laughed. "Oh, I know all about the Sinners," she continued. "Everyone does."

We stood and I waved to the bartender. This time a guy came over instead of the woman from earlier. I settled our bill, then with my palm against her lower back I escorted her out of *Embers*. We made our way across the street, to the parking lot, then to her car.

When she faced me, the smile on her face made me realize I wanted more from her than I even realized. I'd been infatuated with women before. However, this wasn't infatuation. It wasn't love either, although I wanted to experience that or something close to it, and I wanted to experience it with Oya.

I wrapped my arms around her waist pulling her closer to me. Her smile widened as she wrapped her arms around my neck. "Where to sexy?"

"How about my place?" My brow arched and she laughed. "Yes, my place. And I want a repeat of what we did at the shop."

"I'm not going to disagree with you about that," I said, chuckling.

"Then, follow me."

CHAPTER FIVE

We stepped into the foyer of the massive two-story brick home in the wealthiest part of the city. I don't know what I expected, but this place seemed so not like her. Over the top was what came to mind.

"I got it in the divorce," she said as she pulled off her heels, and tossed her keys in the large bowl that sat on a table in the foyer. "Not my taste, but my ex-husband liked anything and everything extravagant. Would you like another drink?" she asked as I followed her to the little miniature bar sitting in the corner of the massive living room we'd just entered.

My eyes landed on the huge grey stone fireplace and the piece of artwork hanging above it.

"Is that what I think it is?" I asked, my eyes widened.

She handed me a tumbler of whiskey. I looked back at the painting while taking a sip of the amber liquid.

"Depends." She took a sip of hers. "What do you think it is?"

"A Jackson Pollock original."

"You would be correct." She grabbed my hand and pulled me over to the beige couch sitting in front of the fireplace. "It was a wedding gift from my ex-in-laws. My ex fought for it in our divorce like he did with everything else. But I won it. I'm not a Pollock fan, but I was glad he didn't get his greedy hands on it."

"Your divorce must have been dirty, huh?" I eyed her as she took a huge gulp of liquor, draining the glass.

"It was. I fought for two years, and he fought me every step of the way."

"Why so long?"

"He didn't want to let me go so I could live my life." She sighed. "To be honest our marriage was over long before I filed for divorce. He was leading a double life and when I found out, he gave me a reason to walk away. And nobody walks away from Thomas Williams."

I stiffened. "Congressman Williams?"

"The one and only," she responded, rolling her eyes.

Thomas Williams was a real bastard and a crooked politician. If you gave him enough money, he'd help pass legislation you needed. He was also unstable, greedy, and in the pockets of the Russians and possibly the Bianchis.

"He sounds like a real motherfucker." I drained my glass, then sat it on the coaster on the coffee table.

"He is. However, you live and you learn. I've moved on with my life even if he doesn't agree with me doing so."

I didn't like the sound of that. Was he harassing her?

"What's that mean?"

"He has this wild idea we can work things out. But that ship sailed even if he doesn't want to let me go. The only good thing that came from our relationship was Andrew."

"Your son?"

"Yes. He just turned twenty-five and I couldn't be prouder of the man he's become."

I could hear the pride and love for her son in her voice. Hopefully, whatever this was between us, Andrew would give us his blessing.

"I hate to celebrate someone else's heartbreak but I'm so fucking glad your ex fucked up."

She laughed and it was the most remarkable thing I'd ever heard. At that moment I vowed to keep her smiling and laughing if it was the last thing I did.

"Now tell me about you, Gavin Lawson."

"Are you sure you're ready to hear the truth? It's not pretty."

Now I was nervous. How would she react? Would she want this to continue?

"I always want the truth no matter the consequences."

"Well, I'm twenty-seven, and I've owned Forbidden Ink for three years."

"How did you get into tattooing?"

Here goes nothing.

"I learned in prison."

"Prison?" she asked surprised, shifting in her seat.

"It's not what you think, Oya." I took a deep breath and released it. "I'm going to tell you something no one else knows. No one. Not even my family."

"Why would you tell me?"

"Because I don't want this to give you a reason not to give us a chance. So, I'm willing to let you in on my secret."

"Okay. Tell me what happened."

"I took the rap for my father."

Her brows furrowed. "What do you mean you took the rap for your father?"

"Before I went to prison, I was on my way to becoming a priest if you can believe it." She looked at me wide-eyed. "I know. It's crazy, right? Not the man I am, today. Anyway, I was seventeen, and I'd already been accepted into the seminary."

"What made you want to become a priest?"

"When I was younger, I can remember telling my mother, I wanted to become a priest so I could save my father from Hell. He wasn't the best man. Still isn't. He lies and cheats on my mother, yet she thinks his ass walks on water."

I shook my head trying to push away the memories. There had been times my mother would leave for work when I was younger and as soon as she was out the door, my father would have a woman walking through the same door. No shame. No remorse. I wasn't sure if Reaper and King experienced it, but as soon as I was old enough to realize what was going on, Reaper and King weren't even living at home.

"One day he called me, frantic, saying he needed help," I continued. "My brothers were older, and they were off doing their own thing. Both King and Reaper were deep in the mc world at that point. So, of course, I wanted to help him. Always have. Even now I have to force myself to stay away from him, so I don't slip into old habits of trying to save him."

"I understand. For years I tried to save Thomas, too." She put her hand on top of mine. "You can't save anyone who doesn't want to be saved. It took me years to learn, but I came to accept it."

"That's where I'm at now. Even though my brothers don't understand, it's what I need to do for me." She nodded in agreement. "So anyway, like an idiot, I went to where he was. The worst mistake of my fucking life."

I hated thinking about what I got caught up in. My father didn't care about anyone but himself. Seven years ago, he was in his late fifties and still running the streets. Once he retired, he got worse.

"He beat someone over a bad drug deal. Almost killed them. Witnesses said I was the one who was involved, and he didn't say I wasn't. According to him, since I wasn't an adult, I didn't have a record, and there was no evidence connecting me to the crime I wouldn't be convicted. I believed him." I shrugged. "He was my father. Why wouldn't I? The jury found me guilty of assault with a deadly weapon based solely on eyewitness testimony and sentenced me to fifteen years in prison. I served seven of the fifteen, then I was paroled for good behavior."

"Oh my god, Gavin. I'm so sorry."

"Nothing to be sorry about. I was young and dumb. I learned my lesson. Learned it the hard way. Anyway, there was one good thing that came out of it." She furrowed her brows and I laughed. "Prison is where I learned to tattoo."

"Really?"

"Yeah. Voodoo taught me. He's Angel's half-brother. He's serving life for murder. He took me under his wing, showed me how to tattoo, and the rest is history as they say."

"At least something good came out of a shitty situation. How did you become a Sinner?"

"My brothers. King's the oldest and the President. Reaper's the middle kid and a member. Of course, they didn't want me to join, but I needed to belong to something."

"You needed a family," she said more as a statement than a question.

I nodded. "Does my past make you want to end this?"

She cupped my face. "It was unexpected. Yet, I can't say that it changes anything on my end. On the other hand, I'm not so sure I'm thinking straight when it comes to you either."

I pulled her in my lap so she could straddle me. She rubbed my head while I kneaded her ass. "I don't think I'm thinking straight either, but I want this with you for however long you're willing to have me, Oya."

I leaned in and captured her bottom lip between my teeth, slightly biting down on the soft flesh. She groaned against my mouth. Releasing her lip, my tongue explored her mouth. The caress of her lips along with the movement of her body rubbing against my growing erection set my body on fire. I wanted nothing more but to sink inside her and feel her warmth and wetness against me again.

"You feel so good, baby," I moaned. "I want to fuck you, Oya. I want you to cum all over my dick."

"Gavin," she groaned.

She pulled her dress over her head, then tossed it on the floor. I lifted her to where I could unbutton my fly. I raised my hips, then pulled my jeans and boxers down. My erection flung flee and she eyed my cock again.

"Did these hurt?" she asked, running her fingers along my piercings. I shuddered. Anytime I got an erection, they became really sensitive.

"Yes," was my only response before I grabbed her hips and slammed her down on my cock.

"Gavin!" she screamed, but I wasn't going to show her any mercy. I was going to fuck her senseless.

"Fuck you feel good," I groaned, digging my fingers into the flesh of her hips, moving her up and down my shaft. "I'm gonna fuck you until you scream my name, Oya. Then I'm going to fuck you again."

"Oh fuck!" she shouted, her nails piercing the flesh of my shoulders.

I slapped her ass as she bounced on my cock, her head thrown back in passion. With my bottom lip pulled between my teeth, I maneuvered her body, her arousal coating my cock. My grunts and her yelps of pleasure filled the large living room.

She was so fucking beautiful. If I could take a picture, I would. "You're fucking mine, Oya." I slammed her down hard on my cock. She looked at me and whatever she saw in my eyes caused hers to widen. "Do you hear me? Mine. Now fucking come for me."

Her eyes rolled, and her glorious cunt clamped down around me when she came.

"Shit!" I groaned.

Tingles shot from the tips of my toes, then covered my entire body. I released inside her, my body shuddering as she pulled me over the edge. Her sweaty body slumped against mine as we both tried to catch our breaths.

I kissed her forehead and ran my fingers up and down her back. "You make an old woman feel like the only woman in the world, you know that?" she mumbled.

I chuckled. "You are far from being old." She raised her head and looked me in the eye. "And you're the most gorgeous woman I've ever had the pleasure of meeting."

"You are one of a kind, Gavin."

"Nah. I just know a remarkable woman when I see one."

The smile that moved across her face could make a grown man cry. I don't see how anyone in their right mind wouldn't do right by her.

"You want to stay the night?"

I smiled. "I thought you'd never ask."

· · · • • • • • · · ·

I'd never slept so damn good in my entire life. I ran my hands across her silken belly.

"Hmm…" Her eyes slowly peeled open, and she graced me with that smile I was becoming accustomed to. "Good morning," she said in a sleepy voice.

"Good morning, sexy." I pecked her on the lips. "What do you have planned for today?"

She shrugged. "On Sundays, I usually hang out around the house, and grade papers. What about you?"

"I have to go to the shop. I want you to come with me, so I can get your tattoo done."

"I wouldn't be putting you out or anything?"

I rolled on top of her, pushing her legs apart, and settling in between them. "No. I have a slot open this morning." I ran my tongue over the seam of her lips. She moaned, her nails digging into the muscles of my back.

"If you keep doing that, there's no way we're gonna make it to your shop," she said.

I pulled her lip between my teeth, slightly biting down on the flesh. "Gavin," she murmured when I backed away, trailing kisses down the column of her slim neck, across her collarbone. Before I descended further down her body, excessive banging on the downstairs door and ringing of the doorbell filtered through the room.

"What the hell!"

I rolled off her. "You expecting anybody?"

"No." She gazed at the wall above a vanity on the far wall. "Especially, not at seven thirty in the morning."

She groaned, swinging her legs over the edge of the bed. She slid on open-toe black slippers, stood, and covered herself in a large black silk robe. While she walked out of the bedroom, I went into the bathroom, pissed, and washed my hands. When I walked back into the bedroom, I heard arguing. I rushed to get dressed. I didn't know what the hell was going on, but Oya sounded angry, then panicked.

Rushing out of her bedroom, and down the stairs, my vision turned red. Thomas Williams tightly gripped Oya's arm. His face was red, and inches from hers. While she wasn't backing down from him, he had at least fifty pounds on her and towered over her. She tried to slap him, but he caught her wrist.

"Hey!" I yelled, stalking closer to them. He dropped her arms, glaring at me over her head. "What the fuck do you think you're doing, motherfucker?"

"It's fine, Gavin. Thomas was just leaving."

"I'm not going any fucking where," he sneered, never taking his eyes off me. "And who the hell are you and what are you doing in my fucking house with my wife?"

My jeans hung low on my hips and my feet were bare. His eyes flickered down to my shirtless chest, where Sin City MC was tattooed across it before going back to my face. Before I could answer Oya stalked towards the door, then opened it.

72

"Who he is and what he's doing here is none of your damn business. This is my damn house, Thomas. Not yours! Now if you don't leave now, I'm calling the cops."

Thomas Williams' attention jerked towards her. "And tell them what Oya? Do you think they will believe you?" He laughed. "You quickly forget, who I am."

"Get out, Thomas! I'm not going to tell you again."

He looked between me and her, then focused back on me. "You haven't heard the last of me." He pointed at me. "Stay away from my wife or I'm coming after you and your club."

I stepped in front of him, standing mere inches from his face. "Sinners don't take kindly to threats, Congressman. So, I suggest you choose your next steps and words wisely."

He took a step back, then turned on his heels. "This isn't over!" he shouted over his shoulder as Oya slammed the door behind him as he left.

She leaned against the closed door with her eyes closed. I slowly walked towards her and checked her wrists and arms for bruises. "I'm fine." I kissed her forehead when she looked into my eyes. "You shouldn't make an enemy of him," she warned.

"I'm a Sinner, Oya. He shouldn't make an enemy of me."

CHAPTER SIX

Clubhouse

I sat in one of the chairs opposite King while Reaper sat to my left in the clubhouse office. I hated bringing this to them, but I didn't have a choice. I had a run-in with a sitting congressman. A congressman who was in bed with the Russians and the Italians. This shit could come back on the club.

"Before you blow your fucking top, I'm going to start by saying it couldn't be avoided." I planted my forearms on my thighs. "If it could have, I would have."

King looked at me impatiently. I understood he was under pressure. We were trying to keep two women safe from the Bianchi Syndicate. While I hated to add to that pressure, it couldn't be helped.

"Why don't you start from the beginning," Reaper said. "Then we'll go from there."

"I met somebody."

"And that's a problem?" King asked as he leaned back in his office chair.

"It may cause problems with the club."

King narrowed his eyes. "What kind of problems."

"She happens to be the ex-wife of Thomas Williams."

"Who?" Reaper asked, looking between King and me.

"Congressman Williams," I responded. "You know the piece of shit the Bianchi's and the Petrovas have in their pocket. He came by her home this morning while I was there, and he casually threatened me and the club."

"Son of a bitch, Gavin!"

"Fucking hell," Reaper murmured.

"Look. They aren't even fucking together anymore, King. I like her. I like her a lot and I don't give a fuck what any of you got to say about it."

"Does she know your history?" King asked and I scoffed.

"You really do think I'm a piece of shit, don't you?" I shot to my feet. "Look I just thought you should know what's going on."

"Sit down, Gavin," Reaper tossed his hands in the air. "We need a plan if something comes up with this. Not only is Williams a politician, but he's also a dirty one. That can cause problems."

I sighed and plopped back in the seat. "That's why the hell I came. I recognized his name."

"Oya? That's her name?" King asked and I nodded. "And she knows you're a Sinner?"

I sighed. "Of course, King. Despite what you seem to think about me, I wouldn't keep shit like that from her."

"Gavin, I'm not saying anything like that. But with your background and being a Sinner, I don't want you to jump feet first into something and bring along an innocent woman with you."

"What he's trying to say," Reaper said cutting in, "is we're just worried about you. You told me a little about this woman and you seem invested. We don't want you to get hurt."

"I'm not a fucking kid anymore. I can handle my own life." I took in a deep breath and released it trying to calm myself down. "Look if shit starts going down, it could be this. I just thought you might like to know." I stood and walked to the door. "I've got to go. I got an appointment."

"Bring her by," King ordered. "We need to discuss this situation."

"I'll see if she has time."

"Tell her to make time, Gavin," King said. "The fucking club could be affected. It's not a request."

I opened the door and walked out without looking back.

CHAPTER SEVEN

I cleared my calendar. This day had been a long time in the making. Apparently, her son

Andrew was just as busy as me and today we both had a rare day off. I knew absolutely nothing about Andrew Williams only that his mother loved him to death and believed he was the perfect kid. I hated to tell her, no kid was perfect, especially a grown-ass man.

"What did you tell him?" I asked.

"That I met this wonderful man, and I wanted him to meet him. He joked about how he was ready to meet his new dad."

I groaned, shaking my head. "Oh, God."

Her laughter sounded like music to my ears. I was glad she was calm about this situation because I was going fucking insane. Even though we hadn't been dating long we knew whatever this was it was something special despite the age gap between us. Although looking for the approval of a twenty-six-year-old, someone who was only a few years younger than me, to continue to date his mother fucking sucked, I'd do it ten times over if it meant Oya would be in my life forever.

How in the hell is he going to take it?

"I've never been so fucking nervous in my life."

"You're going to be fine, Gavin." She squeezed my hand. "Everything is going to be fine. As long as I'm happy, Andrew will be happy too."

"That's easy for you to say. He's going to love you regardless. If he doesn't like me, where does that leave us?"

I would never push Oya to pick me over her son. I had a lot riding on this introduction. We both did. I wanted to have a long-term relationship with this woman. I could actually see marriage in the future for us. But I knew I couldn't have that unless her adult son was onboard with this.

Can he get past the age gap?

Before she had the chance to answer me, the doorbell to her home sounded. She kissed me on the lips, and before I could deepen it to calm my nerves, she pulled away, then rushed to the front door. She said it had been almost six months since they had seen one another. Apparently, he didn't live in California, but in New England. Their muffled voices and laughter sounded from the foyer.

When he walked in, I stood up, wiping my hands on my blue jeans. My eyes widen when I saw exactly who Oya's son was. "Oh, my fucking God," I mumbled. "You've got to be fucking kidding me."

This is not going to be fucking good.

Andrew's eyes snapped to me, and he stopped in his tracks. I watched every emotion move across his face, from confusion to anger and everything in between.

"Saint?" he called out, anger settling back on his features. "Man, what the fuck?"

"Drew, I didn't know man," I said, shaking my head, holding my hands up when he rushed towards me.

"Wait, Andrew!" Oya shouted.

She stood in between us before Andrew or Drew as I knew him reached me. Andrew fucking Williams, Super Bowl Champion and one of the most well-known linebackers in the NFL was about to try to whip my ass for fucking his mother. This fucking day couldn't get any worse.

"You know Gavin?" Oya asked.

"You fucking my Ma!" he yelled, ignoring his mother's question.

"Andrew!" Oya shouted, getting his attention. "Watch your mouth!"

He sighed, took a step away from us, and started to pace. He was enraged and looked like he was trying his hardest to control his temper. I get it but I'd have no trouble defending myself. Hopefully, it wouldn't come to that.

Oya faced me, her eyes wide, full of questions.

"I've known Drew for a while. He comes in the shop whenever he's in town."

He stopped pacing and glared at me. "How long has this been going on?"

"Not long," Oya replied. "Sit down, so we can talk."

"I don't want to talk about this bullshit," he said. "He's my fucking age, Ma. You can't be serious?"

"I know how old he is. And I don't give a damn if you don't want to talk. I. Said. Sit."

Andrew glared at Oya, and it took all I had not to step in. There was enough tension in this room because of me but it was hard for me to watch him not respect his mother enough for us to have this conversation.

I'd known Drew for a while. He was one of my high-profile clients. Whenever he was in town he'd come into the shop, get some work done, and we'd shoot the shit. He was a good guy from what I could tell and on a couple of occasions, he'd even talked about Oya and never about his father. I guess I knew the reason for that omission. But at the time, I didn't know it was her, but I knew he loved his mother. I didn't blame him for being upset because he wasn't expecting me to be the one dating his mother. He was in shock.

"Now, Andrew!" She pointed to the loveseat.

He huffed and dropped into the loveseat. I'd laugh if this wasn't a serious matter. To see a woman put this big ass man in his place was wild. Oya took a seat on the couch, and I sat beside her. She grabbed my hand and we looked at each other. I gave her a small nod to start. Drew was her kid. He needed to hear things from her, not the man she was fucking.

Oya sighed. "You two know each other, so no introductions are needed. Gavin and I are seeing each other. Because you are the most important person in my life, I thought you should know things are serious."

"Be fucking for real right now, Ma," Drew said, planting his forearms on his thighs. "Do you even know who he is?"

By the look on Oya's face, I could tell she was trying her best to maintain composure with Drew. She loved him and she wanted him to know things were serious between us. At least we weren't doing this shit behind his back. But she didn't like how he was talking to her, and I didn't either.

She took a deep breath and exhaled, trying to calm her anger. "I do." His brows bunched in confusion like there was no way she knew everything about me and still chose to be with me. Even though she knew more about me than my own family. "I know everything."

It wasn't a secret I was a Sinner, and it wasn't a secret I was an ex-con. Most of my clients knew that part of my history. I understood why Drew needed to make sure his mother knew, but that let me know he didn't think too much of me if he thought I'd keep that from her.

"She knows, I'm a Sinner." He glared at me, and I ignored it. "She also knows I was in prison, and she knows why. No one else does. So, whatever you think you know about me, let that shit go, Drew. I'm your tattoo artist. We aren't friends but we're not strangers either. You don't know my personal life just like I don't know yours."

He looked at his mother. "Does Dad, know?"

Oya rolled her eyes. "Of course, he does. He showed up here unannounced one morning."

"Morning?" he sneered.

"Yes, Andrew." She shook her head. "One morning your father showed up and pushed his way into the house. Gavin was here."

The disgust on his face made me chuckle and Oya glared at me causing it to die immediately. I'd be just as disgusted thinking about my mother fucking someone but from the outside looking in it was funny as hell.

"You know he's not going to deal with this in a good way, Ma. Are you ready for the fallout?"

"I can't live my life around your father, Andrew." She pinched the bridge of her nose. "At this point, I don't care what he thinks. I want to be happy. I've moved on and so should he."

"She'll be protected," I said, interjecting. "Your father knows who the Sinners are, and we know who he is."

I wasn't sugarcoating shit for him. His father was just as much of a criminal as me—as the Sinners. His father was no better despite the stuffy designer three-piece suits he wore. If he wanted to use my past as a reason for not getting behind this relationship, then I'd spill all his father's dirty secrets to prove my point. I wasn't going anywhere unless Oya made that decision.

"I want you to be happy for me, son." She looked at me, squeezed my hand, then looked back at Drew. "For the first time in a long time, I'm happy and it's because of Gavin. I know it's going to take some time to get used to."

"Understatement of the year," he mumbled.

"But I want your blessing for me to move on with my life," she said, ignoring his comment, "with Gavin."

"I'm not going to hurt your mother, Drew. I've been completely upfront about who I am and about my past. I'm not trying to pull the wool over her eyes about the man that I am and will always be. I just want the chance to be with the one person who has made me look at life differently. And I want the chance to make her happy. She deserves it and so do I."

He leaned back on the loveseat and looked at me. He was making his decision whether he'd be onboard. We'd spent hours talking about politics, everyday shit, and family at Forbidden Ink. Deep down despite my past, Drew knew I wouldn't hurt his mother. Or at least I thought he knew that I wouldn't.

"You hurt her, and you'll have to deal with me," he said.

"I'd expect nothing less."

CHAPTER EIGHT

CLUBHOUSE

"Alana, what the hell is going on!"

Oya stood beside me with her eyes as big as fucking saucers. What a way to make a first impression of the clubhouse, with what was going on, it wasn't pretty. I'd hoped to ease her into it, but I guess that wasn't going to happen.

Alana had just burst through the office door like a bull in a China shop cursing like a damn sailor. She was fucking furious. I knew King would eventually fuck up. He was a control freak and Alana was far from someone who could be controlled. Like I told him when he first saw her, she was going to be trouble, and this was what I meant. He'd met his match. She wasn't going to put up with his shit and let him walk all over her because he couldn't control what she did.

"Your fucking brother is what's going on."

I sighed. "Anything I can do to help?"

"I'm sure he's been this way his entire fucking life." She rubbed her temples. "There's probably no changing him now. Fucking control freak," she muttered.

I chuckled. "This is Oya, my girlfriend," I said, trying to change the subject. Maybe that would calm her down, so she didn't kill my brother. "Can she hang out with you while I talk to King?"

Alana's eyes widen. "Oh, my god. I'm so sorry, I didn't see you standing there. That man has me so fucking angry."

Oya laughed. "It's all right." She stuck out her hand to Alana and she grasped it. "I'm Oya Williams."

"Alana Robinson." Alana faced me. "Tell him to get a fucking grip, Gavin. Before I shove his balls down his throat."

Without another word, she guided Oya through the crowds of brothers and club whores to the back patio. I'd already explained before we got here the things she might see. But I saw her looking around at all the shit the boys were involved in, and I have no doubt we'd have a long conversation about it when we left. It was just another day at the clubhouse. Half-naked women. People fucking, drinking, and smoking. It was the usual thing that happened here. It was something she'd be around whenever we were here, and I'd be around when here alone. I thought she could handle it, but it would take some time to get used to.

When they stepped outside and closed the door behind them, I pushed open the door to King's office. I didn't know what to expect but it wasn't this. He was going berserk. Right at that moment realization hit me. Alana Robinson meant a hell of a lot to my big brother probably more than he knew. We didn't get along. It had been a long time since we understood each other but watching him destroy his office because of a woman told me all I needed to know about the impact she had on him.

"HEY! Dylan!"

He was so enraged he didn't even know I'd come into the room. When he looked up at me, he tossed the binder in his hand on the desk, then dropped into the chair.

"What the hell is going on?" I asked, picking up some of his papers from the floor and tossing them on the desk in front of him. "We can hear you two yelling through the whole damn clubhouse."

"She's driving me fucking nuts." He ran his hand through his hair. "She's trying to get herself fucking killed."

I sighed and sat in the only chair he hadn't broken. "This about her disappearing?"

My fucking heart sunk when I realized Alana had slipped out the back exit that some of my celebrity clients used whenever they were at the shop. No one had come in and taken her so that left the only other option– she slipped out the back of her own free will.

I was mad as hell. And my brother had every right to be furious too. She was under our protection, and no one had any clue what happened to her. Leaving me with no other choice but to call King and let him know she was missing.

"It's more than that. She met with Messina's brother."

"You've got to be fucking kidding."

No wonder he was losing his shit. If Oya went to meet with her ex-husband and I knew absolutely nothing about it, I'd lose my fucking mind. I'd tear this city apart looking for her because the men both these women were dealing with were dangerous, whether they recognized the threat or not.

"I wish I was."

"What the hell was she thinking?"

I couldn't imagine why she thought anything good would come from putting herself in danger. If anything would have happened to her, she would have started a war between the mafia and the Sinners. Many people would have died or ended up in jail.

"I have no fucking clue. He wants to use her as bait."

"Bait?"

"So, he can kill his brother."

"And she actually believes him?" I scoffed, shaking my head. "If it's true, that's one fucked up family."

We had a fucked-up family. And as much as I bumped heads with both my brothers there was no way in hell, I'd ever harm them. I'd die for them before I killed them.

"Tell me about it." He sighed. "I'm so ready for all this shit to be over. I'm getting too old for all this bullshit."

He leaned back in his chair, then propped his feet up on his desk. This was the first time in a long time, I'd seen my brother stressed the fuck out over this club. He ran it with an iron fist, and it seemed to come naturally. I'd never seen him lose his shit like this until today. I guessed that was what a man in love looked like when his woman put everyone else's safety above their own.

"We got to deal with Savage Order, possibly your woman's ex, and the damn Bianchi's. For once I'd like to have a day when we're not dealing with bullshit."

I hated to break the news to him but that definitely wasn't going to happen when you're a part of this world. But he already knew that, and I learned that lesson early on. There was always an issue with something. And as Prez, it was up to him to deal with it.

"Anyway," he continued, "I know you're not here to listen to me bitch about shit that's not going to change. What's up?"

"Oya's here."

"Are you sure about this woman, little brother?"

I frowned. I'd tried to maintain my composure when he or Reaper questioned what the hell I was doing with my life. They still treated me like I was a kid even though I'd lived a hard life. Seven years in fucking prison wasn't a cakewalk. I knew when I wanted something.

I wasn't perfect by no means but goddamn it, I wasn't a child who was thinking with his dick instead of my fucking brain.

He threw up his hand stopping me before I could respond. "I'm not questioning your decision, Gavin." He heaved a sigh. "I just want you to be prepared for what's coming. If this is the woman you want, I'll back you. But be sure because not only does this relationship affect you, but it also affects this club whether you believe it or not."

"I want her, Dylan." I shrugged.

There wasn't anything I was more sure of as I was of that. Oya was mine and nothing or no one would stop me from being with her including King and this club. "Of course, I don't want to involve the club, but it is what it is. She's mine and I'm a Sinner until I die. There's no separating the two."

"Well, then if she's your woman, that's all I need to hear. Go get her and let me meet her."

I smiled which was something I didn't do much of until Oya walked into Forbidden Ink. She made me happy and no matter who I had to destroy to keep her in my life that was what would be done.

I nodded then left his office to find Oya.

CHAPTER NINE

Her moans went straight to my cock.

We'd spent most of our time going back and forth from work and checking up on King and Alana. I still couldn't believe that her ex tried to kill her. If it hadn't been for the quick thinking of my brother, Messina would probably have gotten away.

Yesterday when we left the hospital, we decided I'd crash at her house for the weekend. We hadn't spent as much time together as I'd like, with her job, my business, and now this shit with Alana. But I needed her as much as I needed air to breathe. She was my calm amidst the storm.

I felt completely helpless as my brother lost his shit about the woman he refused to say he loved. But when I was with Oya everything felt right with the world even though in reality none of that was true. Alana was fighting for her life. And Oya's ex was still looking to take the Sinners down which King said we wouldn't have to deal with much longer.

It wasn't that I didn't trust my brother. I didn't trust Emilio Messina to deal with Williams. Of course, Messina owed the Sinners. King had killed his brother, something he failed to do which almost cost Alana her life. But if King believed Messina was good for it, I'd believe it until I didn't. Then I'd have no other choice but to do it myself.

Her hands grasped my head as I circled her swollen clit with the tip of my tongue. Being between her thighs was like heaven. My safe place. Going to sleep and waking up with the taste of her arousal on my tongue was the most exhilarating thing I'd experienced in a long time. Never had a woman captured my attention like Oya. If it was the last thing I did, I would make her my wife.

"Gavin," she moaned, the scent of her arousal mixing with the sound of us making love filled the room.

We'd only had a few hours of sleep because my dick couldn't help but find a home inside her warm cunt most of the night and into the early morning hours. And when I woke up this morning to her luscious body snuggled up against mine, and my dick laying snuggly against the crack of her ass, I couldn't help myself. I gently rolled her onto her back, making sure not to wake her up until my tongue was buried deep inside her pretty cunt.

"Good morning, babe," I said against her wet folds.

Her body shivered and I smirked. Oya's responsiveness to my touch was one thing that made me want to fuck her all the time.

That kind of responsiveness made a man's ego blow the fuck up. I couldn't stop touching her, smelling the alluring scent of her skin, the tempting fragrance of her cunt. The woman was fucking addictive.

"Fuck, baby," she groaned, riding my mouth. "Keep doing that. Right there."

I hummed, lifted her legs over my shoulders, then sucked her clit into my mouth, pushing two fingers inside her tight pussy.

"Gavin!" she shouted as I moved my fingers in and out of her, quickening my pace.

I alternated between flicking and sucking her clit, while continuing to drive my fingers in and out of the channel, pushing her closer to the edge. Her legs tightened around my head as she rocked her hips, finding the rhythm she needed to come.

My fucking cock was hard as steel. I couldn't wait to sink inside her, but I loved eating her pussy so much that I wanted to drag this out for as long as I could. But I didn't think she would be able to hold on much longer. Her grip on my head tightened as she moved my head in sync with the movement of her hips.

"I'm coming!" She tried to push me away, but I gripped her thighs tighter, making sure I sucked her clit harder while she came undone. "Fuck! Fuck! Fuck!"

Her delicious nectar flooded my mouth and my eyes rolled. Jesus fucking Christ, I'd never known a woman's pussy to taste as good as Oya's. It was hard to describe the taste. Something sinful, sexy, and downright intoxicating would be the best description. And I absolutely could not get enough of it.

When her thighs and hands loosened on my head, I gave her cunt one final long lick from her entrance to her swollen nub causing her beautiful body to tremble.

Settling in between her legs, she gave me the same look she always gave me since we'd been fucking. Like she couldn't believe my dick was pierced and I was going to fuck her with it.

I chuckled. "What's that look for baby girl." I pumped my hard cock, enjoying the fear, disbelief, and lust swirling in her eyes. "You know how good these feel inside your tight pussy, relax and let me in."

"I can't believe, I'm letting you fuck me with your mechanical dick," she said, spreading her legs wider despite her words.

"You love my mechanical dick, and you know it."

My eyes dropped to her pussy, covered in her cum and my spit. Was it possible for a woman to have a beautiful cunt? If it was, Oya's would win the top prize. It was gorgeous. Taste, smell, and the way it shifted from deep dark brown to pink. Mother. Fucking. Beautiful.

I didn't wait for her to tell me how much she loved my dick, I just slammed into her. She knew she was about to reach fucking nirvana with this mechanical dick, as she liked to call it.

"Fuck you feel, like fucking heaven, Oya." I deepened my thrust, relishing in the soft, velvety feel of her warm channel snuggly wrapped around my cock. "I'm going to fuck you until the day I die, Oya. This pussy is mine. Mine for fucking forever."

My thrusts sped up. Because it was Oya and her magical pussy it didn't take long for me to nut. The melodic sound of my nuts hitting her ass as I pounded into her tight pussy sounded like a damn choir of angels. The tingling of my approaching orgasm started at the tip of my toes like it always did and quickly encompassed my entire being.

"Fuck! Fuck! Fuck!" I yelled, throwing my head back, closing my eyes, and roaring as total fucking bliss covered my entire frame.

Stars danced behind my eyes as her pussy milked me dry. This was how it always was with her. Fucking cosmic.

As soon as I emptied all my cum into her pussy, I pulled out, and settled back between her legs, gathering our mixed arousal on my tongue.

I groaned. This was also one of my favorite flavors. The mixture of her cum and mine. I sucked on her clit, giving it a few hard pulls before I gathered our cum on my tongue and rose between her legs.

She eyed me hungrily, watching my every move. I settled above her body then my mouth crashed onto hers. I pushed my cum covered tongue in her mouth so she could taste how well we went together. There was no better flavor than us.

She groaned into my kiss, hungrily taking everything, I gave her with just as much passion. When I pulled away her eyes were glazed over, her body covered in sweat, and she looked thoroughly fucked. I loved every bit of it. Just thinking about how well she took my cock had my dick swelling again.

"Why are you looking at me like you want to fuck me again?" she asked with a smirk. She knew I couldn't get enough of her.

My dick nudged at her entrance. "Maybe because I do," I replied, sliding back home. "I'm never letting you go, Oya."

She wrapped her legs around my hips. "Are you sure about that?""Never. You're stuck with me and my mechanical dick forever."

CHAPTER TEN

I paced my office at Forbidden Ink as Oya looked at me like I'd lost my mind. This was at least the fucking third time her ex had tried to confront her. Once when I was there and another time while she was out with Raquel, now at her job.

This shit had to end. I've been patiently waiting for Emilio Messina, the new Don of the Bianchi Syndicate to do what he promised King he'd do, but he wasn't moving fast enough for me. Now Oya's job was in jeopardy because her damn ex-husband didn't know how to take no for an answer and move on with his life.

"This is fucking ridiculous!" I stopped pacing and looked at her. "He shouldn't be able to do this."

She sighed after I resumed pacing. "I agree. But power and money talk, and unfortunately, he has both. I'm not worried Gavin, the truth will eventually come out. Everything will be all right."

That motherfucker had the nerve to approach the Dean of the university with the outrageous allegation accusing Oya of giving grades in exchange for money. Now the school was investigating and had put her on unpaid leave indefinitely.

"He's costing you your job." I shook my head in disbelief at how far he was willing to go. I shouldn't be surprised because he was a bastard but Oya's the mother of his kid. You think that meant something but if that didn't mean anything to my father why would it mean anything to someone like the congressman. "And for what? Because of me?"

If I had anything fragile in my vicinity, I'd break it. I was so fucking pissed. Not only was he going after the Sinners' legal businesses, including Forbidden Ink, but now he was going after her job too.

It hadn't even been two hours since the Health Department had left because someone had filed a complaint against us. Of course, they didn't find shit because there was nothing to find. I did shit the way it was supposed to be done because this place was my life. If it got out that a complaint had been filed about Forbidden Ink being unsanitary, I could be ruined. Not only my business but me as a tattoo artist. I wouldn't be able to work again. Which I knew was what he wanted. He wanted to hit me and the Sinners.

Oya stood and walked to me, causing me to stop pacing. She cupped my face. "We will get through this, okay?" She kissed my lips and then pulled away. "Take a breath."

I closed my eyes, inhaled a deep breath, then released it opening my eyes. "I'm sorry."

I can't imagine how this was impacting her. We just wanted to be happy. I finally found contentment and some asshole was doing everything in their power to destroy it. What sucked was someone else was handling him when it should be me. I didn't give up easily and I wouldn't this time, but it wasn't easy. None of this should be as hard as it was.

Her brows dipped in confusion. "For what?"

"For bringing all this down on you. I don't want our relationship to cost you everything you've worked hard for."

She wrapped her arms around my neck. "This isn't anyone's fault, but Thomas'. Everything will work out. Trust me."

Before I could respond, there was pounding on my office door. "Police!"

"Police," I muttered as I walked to the door. "What the hell?"

I yanked the door open. Two uniformed officers stood there like they were ready for anything. My eyes flicked down to their hands on the butts of their guns, then back to their eyes.

"Can I help you?" I asked as calmly as possible. I wasn't about to get shot by police officers who were ready to kill me on the spot.

"Are you Gavin Lawson?" the officer who was closest to me.

"I am."

"We have a warrant for your arrest," he said, while the other officer pulled out his handcuffs. "Please turn around and put your hands behind your back."

"What for?" Oya asked. "Let me see the warrant."

"Ma'am. Step back."

"But he didn't do anything!" she shouted.

I was so fucking overjoyed she had so much faith in me. I hadn't done anything, and it felt amazing to have someone on my side especially when this was about to be a shit fest.

"It's fine, babe." I turned around and put my hands behind my back. "I didn't do anything so there's nothing to worry about."

I hated the tears pooled in her eyes. She was scared for me. But I was used to these types of situations. I'd spent the best years of my life in prison. There was no reason for me to freak out because I wasn't a kid anymore and I wouldn't make the same mistakes I'd made back then.

"Call Reaper. Tell him what's happened," I said as the cops escorted me out of my office.

Thank God today was slow, and the shop was empty right now. I could possibly lose customers if they'd seen me being ushered out in handcuffs despite it all being bullshit.

"What the fuck, Gav?" Angel asked as we passed him.

"I don't know, man. Cancel the rest of my appointments, and give Oya, Reaper's number."

"What about King?" Angel asked from behind me.

"Don't bother him. He needs to be with Alana."

My older brother had enough shit to deal with. All I needed was for Reaper to get in touch with our lawyer and let him handle the rest because I know for a fact, I haven't done shit.

"I got you," Angel said. "Hang in there until the cavalry arrives."

"Don't worry, Oya!" I shouted as they pushed me out the front door. "Everything's going to be fine."

· · • • · ♦ • · · ·

Handcuffed to a metal bar bolted to a green rectangular table in an interrogation room was like deja vu. It wouldn't shock me if this was the same room I was in all those years ago. My much younger self freaked out when this happened before. Seven years in prison and running with the Sinners had hardened me to this type of situation. They wouldn't break me this time because they can't. I wasn't that same kid.

I'd been in here well over an hour. I could feel their eyes burning into my head as they hid behind the one-way window that took up most of the wall in front of me. They thought they could make me sweat. But they weren't going to get anything out of me especially since I hadn't done shit.

The door to the interrogation room swung open and I groaned when two detectives I was very familiar with strolled in the room with smirks on their faces. These were the two detectives who had helped convict me.

"Look who's back," Detective Moore said as he tossed a manila folder on the table then took one of the seats in front of me, while Detective Chavis, took the other. "If it ain't Gavin Lawson, or should I call you Saint."

I rolled my eyes but kept my mouth shut. He could call me whatever the fuck he wanted. I didn't give a fuck and I wouldn't let this prick get under my skin.

"Cat got your tongue?" Detective Moore asked, chuckling.

"Nope." I shrugged like it was no big fucking deal I was here. "I just ain't got shit to say other than, I want my lawyer."

Detective Moore narrowed his eyes at me. He couldn't stand the sight of me. Other than being a Sinner, I didn't know why. When I was arrested at seventeen, I had nothing to do with the club, but he still made it his mission to make sure I went to prison for as many years as possible for the charge. If I didn't know any better, it was personal, and he held a grudge against me. I didn't know him personally, so I didn't know why he had a hard-on for me.

"You're no better than your father," he sneered.

And there it was. He knew my Da.

"What did he do?" I asked, not able to stop the smile curving my lips. "Let me guess. Now you tell me if I'm wrong, Detective Moore," I taunted, laughing. "He fucked your wife, didn't he?"

"You son of a bitch! "Detective Moore shouted, as he shot to his feet, then planted his palms on the table. His face was only inches from mine. He didn't deny it so that definitely had to be what this was all about. What a small fucking world. My Da and the detective that helped send me to prison had a fucking history.

"If I know anything about my Da, he probably fucked her in your house." I chuckled. "Am I right? Did you walk in on them together?"

Anger rolled off him, but I didn't give a fuck. I understood he didn't like my Da, but what the hell did that have to do with me? Back then I knew these two detectives had it out for me, but I couldn't understand why. I'd even mentioned it to my Da, which evidently was the wrong person to say anything to. But I was a seventeen-year-old kid. A baby who didn't know shit about how the cops operated. And these two used my trust in the police against me. But now I knew how they rolled. It didn't matter if I didn't do shit, they'd find a way to pin it on me anyway. But not this time. Every fucking thing that had gone wrong in my life centered around my fucking sperm donor but this time I would not be the collateral damage to his behavior. I was going home to my woman.

"You're going down, Lawson," Detective Moore threatened. "Just like you did all those years ago."

Once again, the door swung open and the Sinners' lawyer, Johnathan Ledet strolled in. The man had a presence and was a badass in the courtroom. He wasn't around when I got sent up the first time. I was sure if he'd been my lawyer there'd been no way in hell, I would have pulled time. He would have figured out a way to get me off.

He arched his brow. "Gavin, you good?"

"You got here just in time, Johnathan," I said without taking my eyes off the detective. "It looks like Detective Moore has a problem with his temper."

"I see," Johnathan said, eyeing Detective Moore. "Detective, I suggest you get out of my client's face and have a seat unless you want to have a lawsuit on your hands."

He unwillingly pulled his gaze away from me and focused on Johnathan Ledet. The man was one of the most powerful defense attorneys in Oakland, and always got any member cleared of anything they'd been charged with. I wished I'd been a Sinner all those years ago, I know for a fact I never would have served a day in prison.

Ledet took the seat beside me, his six-foot-four frame barely contained in the rickety metal chair. He sat his brown leather briefcase on the floor at his feet. "Sorry it took me so long to get here," he said, apologizing. "I was in court, so it took a while for my assistant to get me the message."

"No worries," I said. I was just grateful he was here now. "I haven't said anything."

"Good."

He turned his attention to the two detectives who were seething in their seats. They knew the reputation of Johnathan Ledet. And they also knew they were fucked. He'd eat them and the fake ass evidence alive.

"So, gentlemen, you don't have a case. My client will not be making a statement at this time."

"You don't know what we have," Detective Moore sneered. "Your client killed a man, and we have an eyewitness to prove it. He's a violent criminal and this time, I'll be putting him in prison for life."

I held in my emotions. I wouldn't let them goad me into showing any anger especially when they'd try to use that outburst against me. There was no fucking way I killed anyone, and I could prove it. I was either at the shop, with Oya, or at the clubhouse. Every place had security footage to prove where I was.

"You have anything to say for yourself?" Detective Chavis asked me.

I looked at my attorney then looked back at Detective Chavis, keeping my mouth shut.

"My client has nothing more to say, and this interview is over."

He leaned over and whispered in my ear, then got up and left. My bond hearing was at nine in the morning, and I'd be home for lunch.

"Take me back to my cell."

CHAPTER ELEVEN

My bond hearing was set not one day after my arrest like Johnathan said but four damn days. He ran into brick wall after brick wall trying to find out why the day had been moved. Four days I had to spend in that godforsaken place before all the evidence my lawyer gave to the detectives and the DA was reviewed then all the charges had been dropped before I'd even made it in front of the judge. There was no way I could have done what they accused me of doing. No doubt Oya's ex-husband was involved. He tried to stonewall my release. The question was why.

Fucking four days of revenue lost because of some bullshit. Four days of my time with Oya, gone.

"How much longer?" I asked.

"Messina said any day now," King responded, rubbing his temples. "He's having to tie up loose ends so none of us go down for this. Killing a sitting congressman can't be done without some planning, little brother."

"I know." I sighed. "I'm just tired of all this shit. If it hadn't been for the surveillance at the shop I turned over and Oya giving the surveillance footage of us entering her house, I'd be in jail again for something I didn't do."

"What the hell, did you just say?" Reaper asked, his brows pulled together in confusion. "In jail for something you didn't do?"

Fuck! I'd been so wound up I didn't even think before I said anything. I was planning on taking that secret to the grave. Just because my relationship with our Da would always be shit that didn't mean their relationship had to be too.

"Never mind."

I hoped they dropped the subject but the way they both glared at me, I wouldn't be that lucky. Fuck! This won't go over good.

I sighed. "If I tell you, you have to promise to let it go. It's done and over with."

"We'll be the ones to decide about that," Reaper said, with his forearms planted on his thighs.

We were at King's. He'd been spending more time at home with Alana than at the clubhouse. She was recovering but it was going slow. And my brother was losing his shit because he wanted her recovery to be quicker, especially with the baby. I couldn't blame him. If Oya was in the same position, I don't think I'd be thinking rationally either.

Kids hadn't been something we'd talked about since we hadn't been seeing each other that long, but I wouldn't mind having at least one. Preferably a son because I do not think I could handle having a daughter, especially in this life. That was if Oya wanted to.

"If I don't have your word, then I'll take it to my grave."

They looked at each other, and I could tell they didn't want to agree to my terms, but they also wanted to know what the hell was going on. I waited patiently for them to make their decision. I wished they'd just let it go but I doubt they would.

"Talk," King said.

"I didn't do what they said I did."

It was better to go ahead and rip the band-aid off.

Their brows dipped in confusion. "What the hell do you mean?" Reaper asked. "You didn't fight it. You didn't tell any of us you were fucking innocent. Why in the hell would you go down for some shit you didn't do?"

"Because Da convinced me I wouldn't get convicted." I leaned back into the couch. "He was the one that did it and convinced me to take the blame. He said I wouldn't get convicted because I didn't have a record, and I was young. And by the time I regretted listening to him, it was too late. I'd been convicted."

They both stared at me with their eyes wide, like I lost my fucking mind. Looking back on it, I probably had. My entire life up until that point had been to help my father become a better man. Even going as far as heading to seminary school to do it because I thought if I became a priest, he'd take my intervention more seriously. Obviously, that was the dream of a kid. My dad didn't want to be saved. He probably still doesn't, and I've learned it wasn't my place to help him. He needed to do that all on his own.

"Are you fucking serious?" Reaper asked, the anger in his voice was almost unbearable to hear.

All I could do was nod. I couldn't tell if he was angry at me or our father. Maybe both of us.

I had no plans on ever telling my brothers the part my father played in my incarceration. While that time of my life had been bad, something useful had come out of it. I learned how to tattoo from one of the greatest to hold a gun. I was able to start my own business, and if I hadn't been in prison, more than likely I'd be trapped being a priest because that wasn't something I wanted to do for myself but for my Da.

"He's fucking dead," King said, jumping to his feet and pacing his living room. "I can't believe he'd do some shit like this! To his own fucking kid!"

I pinched the bridge of my nose. "No."

That stopped him dead in his tracks. "What?" he asked. "What the fuck do you mean no, Saint! Seven fucking years! Seven fucking years he took of your life!"

"You act like I don't know that!" I took in a breath and blew it out, hoping to calm down. I planted my forearms on my knees and looked both my brothers in the eyes. "I said no, King. I don't want either of you to do anything."

They looked at me like I had a third head. "Look. I'm not saying that I've forgiven him because I haven't. I probably never will. But there's no point in hashing this shit out. I've done the time and nothing's going to change that. I keep my distance from him and that's enough for me."

"Why didn't you tell us?" King asked, plopping back down on the couch.

Genuine hurt blanketed his face. And the only answer I had was that I didn't think they'd believe me. It sucked but I wasn't close to him because he was so much older. I was closer to Reaper, but he had his own issues. And there was no fucking way, I'd tell Ma the truth. She believed the sun rose and set in our Da. She'd find a reason to believe him over me. I love my Ma, but she always chose him over us.

"To be honest, I didn't think anyone would believe me."

I held up my hand to stop their protest. I was young. I was going through shit at home with Da while they were out living their lives. I felt abandoned. And all I really had going in my life was my quest to save our Da.

"Young and dumb, bro. I wished I would have said something, but I live with the consequences of my actions every day. I will forever be an ex-con. But I moved forward in my life. I've made something of myself. I don't want to look back. I want to look forward to my future. My future with a remarkable woman. Please just let it go."

If my brothers looked at me like I was a different person that was good enough for me. And to be honest, a heavy weight had been lifted off my shoulders. I felt lighter. Freer. Maybe keeping this secret hadn't been the best thing for me. Maybe it was my last ditch ever to save my father. But it wasn't up to me to save him. I know that now. You can't save someone who doesn't want to be saved. A long hard lesson to learn but at least I learned it.

King stood and walked towards me. When he stood in front of me his face was full of regret. "I'm sorry. I'm so fucking sorry I didn't do more for you. I should have done more."

I stood and gave my brother a hug, then released him. "There wasn't anything you could do, bro. I didn't ask for help. You didn't know I needed it."

He nodded, stepped out of the way, and Reaper took his place. "We should have known your ass couldn't do nothing like that."

I chuckled as he hugged me tightly. When he pulled away, he didn't need to apologize, it was written all over his face just like King's. "We're good," I said, so he didn't have to voice it. Something had changed with my brother when I got sent away. He wasn't the same, but I guess I wasn't either.

King's cell phone rang. He answered and said a few words before he ended the call. He looked at me with a smile on his face. "Messina says it's a go. Congressman Williams will no longer be a problem."

I shouldn't feel elation. I shouldn't feel excited, but I did. I was so glad that motherfucker would meet his end. The only thing I regretted was I wouldn't be the one to do it. It was a difficult decision to make, but I didn't believe Oya or Drew would forgive me if I did it, so I had to settle for Messina getting that honor.

CHAPTER TWELVE

"Fuck Oya," I groaned, gripping her locs tighter. "Shit. Right there, baby."

My cock was encased in her warm, wet mouth, and it felt like fucking heaven. She hummed and the sensation had my fucking toes curling. It took all I had not to set the pace. I wanted to fuck her mouth, so I could fuck her tight cunt, but this was her show. And what a fucking show it was.

Maybe she would let me eat her cunt while she sucked me off? I think that was a good compromise.

I tapped her thigh, and she slowly pulled away from my dick. Her mouth felt remarkable. Not as much as her pussy but it was damn near close.

At first, when she decided to give me a blow job, she had a hard time because of my piercings. She was afraid of hurting me. I didn't know how many times I had to explain to her that she couldn't hurt me by sucking my dick. She finally got more comfortable once she understood there was nothing she could do to cause me any pain, just pleasure. She had gotten used to sucking me off with my piercings and now she did that shit like a pro. Just the right amount of pressure, spit, and roughness. She knew how to make me come faster than anyone had ever done.

"Sit on my face."

"You just won't let me run shit, will you?" she asked, laughing.

"You can run whatever the fuck you like after I eat *my* pussy. Now get that beautiful ass up here and ride my face, baby."

She didn't say anything else and did as I asked. Gripping her hips, I pulled her closer to my mouth, while she engulfed my dick, the tip hitting the back of her throat. She groaned and once again that vibration had my fucking toes curling. If I could eat her pussy for the rest of my life, I'd die a happy and blessed man.

Her body quivered as I devoured her pussy like the Devil would devour a soul.

My fingers dug into the flesh of her hips as she rode my face while giving me one of the best blowjobs in my entire life. Tingling covered my entire body and my hips rose off the bed. "Fuck!" I groaned as I released into her mouth.

Once my dick stopped twitching inside her mouth, she swallowed all my cum and licked my dick clean causing me to shiver. I tapped her thigh. "Hands and knees baby."

"I don't have time, Gavin."

"Where the hell do you think you're going?" I asked when she tried to get up from the bed, but I pulled her back to me.

"I've got to meet, Andrew," she said, giggling when I wouldn't let her pull away from me.

I flipped her over onto her back and thrust inside her. "Gavin!" she shouted.

"We've got time."

I hiked one of her legs over my shoulder and moved in and out of her, deeper and faster, at the angle I knew would make her scream my name. Her nails clawed at my back, and I loved the pain.

"Fuck, Oya. This pussy is so damn good."

Her deep, guttural moans shifted to screams and the sounds of her cries and my balls slapping her ass echoed in the room.

"Oh! Gavin. Fuck! Fuck me!"

I smirked. She looked like she was in fucking heaven. If she was feeling anything like me, this was as close as we'd both get.

I hissed when her nails dug into my shoulders. I was hitting that special spot. Her pussy slickened even more. The walls of her pussy fluttered around my cock until they clamped down around me. I groaned as her arousal dripped down my dick onto my balls.

I quickly pulled back, settled between her thighs, and licked from her entrance to the top of her slit gathering her arousal on my tongue. She wiggled against my mouth as I pulled her sensitive clit inside my mouth and sucked hard, forcing another orgasm to move through her body. She gripped my hair and screamed out my name, flooding my mouth again.

Fuck! I could do this all day if she'd let me. As she came down from her orgasm, I rose from between her legs, leaned forward, and captured her plump lips. This woman was the future. Whether she knew it or not, she was my everything.

She moaned into my mouth as she tasted herself on my tongue. She pulled away from me with heavy-lidded eyes. "You are amazing, Gavin Lawson."

I couldn't help the smile that crossed my face. "So are you, Oya Williams."

She pecked my lips and rolled from under me and jumped off my bed when I tried to deepen the kiss.

"You're insatiable."

"It's all you, baby."

She smiled and it was like everything was right with the world even though it wasn't. Her ex was coming after both of us. Hopefully, Messina would do what he needed to do and then we could move forward in our lives.

"I'm going to take a shower," she said.

"I'll join you."

She shook her head and held her hands out to stop me from getting off the bed. "No. I will never make it to lunch."

"I can be quick," I said.

I could. All I wanted to do was fuck her in the shower. Maybe bend her over and fuck her from behind.

Her eyes widen when they dropped to my dick. I shrugged. I couldn't help it. I wanted to be inside her. She laughed as she dashed to the bathroom, closed the door behind her, and locked it.

I looked at the clock sitting on the nightstand beside my bed. I only had an hour to make it to my appointment, so I guess we really didn't have time to play. I had enough time to take a quick shower and get to the shop, but I still would much rather stay here with her.

"I guess I'm going to the guest bathroom."

CHAPTER THIRTEEN

My last client had already left for today and I was fucking ecstatic. I couldn't wait to get out of here. That had been another thing that had changed since I met Oya. Forbidden Ink had become my home away from home. I spent more time here than anywhere else. Now I couldn't wait until the end of my day when before I wished the days lasted longer.

A knock sounded at the door as I tossed the paper towels, I used to clean, within the trash bin by the door. I pulled it open. I was shocked to see Drew standing there with a look of concern on his face.

"What's wrong?" I asked as my heart sunk to my gut.

"Have you seen my mother? She was supposed to meet me a few hours ago, and she didn't show up."

I pulled out my phone and dialed her number. When it went straight to voice mail concern was replaced with fear. I dialed King next.

"He has her," I said as soon as he answered.

"Who has who?" he asked, his voice sounding full of stress.

I didn't know who else to go to. He had a direct line to Messina who had eyes on Williams. I knew he had her because there was no fucking way she'd stand up to Drew.

"Williams has Oya."

"Let me call you back," King said then ended the call.

"Call your mother, Drew."

He didn't hesitate and tried dialing her while I paced the room. "Voicemail," he said.

"Have you talked to your father?"

"No. We don't talk that much anymore," he confessed. "He only calls when he needs something."

I hated to open old wounds because I could hear the anger and disappointment in his voice. It was a feeling I knew all too well and still tried not to dwell on even though I wasn't a kid anymore. But I'd always feel the disappointment and anger that shit just didn't work out with my father.

"Call him and put it on speaker. I want to hear what he says."

"You think he has her?" he asked.

"I do," I said, pinching the bridge of my nose as I tried to calm the anger and fear moving through me. "There's no fucking way she'd stand you up. Call him."

He nodded and got on the phone with his father, and I'd done something I hadn't done in a long ass time. I prayed. I prayed to whoever would listen to keep her safe at least until I could get there. I was going to kill the motherfucker even if it sent me back to prison. She'd survive this. As long as she didn't have to deal with him anymore, he'd die a thousand deaths.

"Dad. Have you heard from Mom?" Drew asked.

"No, hey Dad. No, how you doing?"

Drew deeply sighed. "I don't have time for pleasantries, Dad. Have you heard from her or not?"

"And why do you think I've heard from her? She doesn't talk to me anymore, especially now that she's fucking that criminal. Do you know who he is, Drew? That fucking bitch left me for some thug."

"I don't have time for the dramatics. I want to know where she is."

There was a moment of silence and I hoped that he'd do the right thing. At least for his son.

"I haven't seen her," he said, then ended the call without another word.

"He's lying," Drew said, running his hand over his head.

I knew he was freaking the fuck out just like me. My cell rang, I grabbed it from the table in the room where I tattooed, and answered without looking at the caller ID.

"Oya?"

"No, it's me, little brother," King said, and my heart dropped. "Good news. Messina knows where she's at. I told him to hold off until you get there. That you'd want to take care of this yourself."

"You damn, right," I said, relief and anger moving through me. "Where?"

"He's holding her in Petrova territory. Where they hold their underground fights. Reaper and Snake are going to meet you there. Messina's men are providing you with anything you need."

"Thanks, bro. I owe you one."

"Don't worry about it. She's a Sinner. She's family."

He ended the call, and I faced Drew. "I know where she's at," I said, rushing to the door.

"I'm going with you."

I stopped him. "You can't. You have too much to lose and if anything happened to you, Oya wouldn't survive it."

"That's my mama, man. I got to help."

"You can't be involved in this man. This isn't going to be a situation where the cops come and save the day. This is going to be dirty. You can't lose everything you've worked for over this."

Resignation crossed his face. "Okay. Just get her home safely."

That was what I planned to do, but I needed to get some things off my chest, and I might not be able to do that with her.

"If I don't make it back, I need you to tell Oya, I love her, and she's been the best thing that's ever happened to me."

He stared at me for a minute but then nodded.

"I'll have her call you when I get her," I said over my shoulder as I raced out the door.

For the first time in a long time, I actually have a clue what was the most important thing in my life. I didn't feel lost anymore. Oya was my saving grace and if I died today, I would die knowing that I had finally found the one for me. My other half. The person I'd love in this life and the next.

CHAPTER FOURTEEN

I made it to the Petrova's territory in no time. It was in one of the seedier parts of Oakland all the criminal elements of this town did business.

The Petrovas ran an underground fighting operation. It was one of those things everyone knew about but they didn't talk about, so I had no trouble finding it.

By the time I pulled up a block away from where the motherfucker was holding Oya. Reaper and Snake were already there waiting. As soon as I parked my bike alongside them, a blacked-out Mercedes crept up beside us.

Without hesitating, all three of us pulled our guns and pointed them at the back window as it rolled down.

"Calm down." He looked at us and smirked. "We're on the same side."

"I seriously fucking doubt that," Reaper sneered.

The man chuckled. "I'm Don Emilio Messina."

"I know who you are," I said. "But we're not putting the guns away."

He looked at me then shrugged. "It doesn't matter. Whatever makes you feel better. Anyway, I worked out a deal with the Petrovas. You'll get no interference from them. Do what you have to do, and I'll clean the mess up."

"And why should we trust you?" I asked. "You're heading the Bianchis. We're not on the same side."

"I'm a man of my word. King did me a favor and now I'll do one for him. The congressman is on the first floor of the first building on the corner of the intersection with your woman."

He started to roll up the window, then stopped. "Tell King, we're even," he said, then rolled the window up before the car drove off.

We watched as the car reached the intersection and went in the opposite direction of where Oya was being held.

"We gonna trust him?" Snake asked.

"If it goes left, King will take care of it," Reaper said.

"You guys don't have to do this. I can get her by myself."

"Shut the fuck up, kid," Snake said, checking the magazine of his gun before pushing it back in. "Let's go get your girl."

I smiled. This was what brotherhood was. We came together when shit was bad and when we needed each other. I was grateful.

When we entered the building as quietly as possible. I was surprised we didn't have to break in which showed how comfortable

Williams was with the Petrovas that he didn't make sure they had his back.

It had been known in the mc underworld the congressman's hands were as dirty as you could get if you were on the right side of the law. But we didn't have any dealings with him because of his connections with human trafficking. We were all criminals but that was one thing the Sinners weren't involved with.

Williams' voice echoed throughout the first floor. We didn't exactly know where on the first floor he was holding Oya, but it had to be towards the back of the building. Her groans, yelps, and his curses filled the empty space.

Moving as quietly as possible without alerting him he wasn't alone, we quickly moved towards where we thought he might be holding her. Once we reached the back of the building there was a long hallway.

"He's got to have her in one of the rooms," Snake whispered.

Reaper and me both nodded.

Oya's screams tore through my soul, and I took off in a full run. I heard Reaper curse under his breath, but I didn't give a fuck. She was hurting and I had to get to her. I didn't care if he heard me coming.

"Thomas don't do this," she pleaded.

"Fuck you, bitch!" he screamed.

I reached the last door on the left in the hallway right before the exit. Hearing Oya's voice in so much pain was a relief and angered me so much that I saw red. I was relieved she was alive. Fucking angry that this bastard had the fucking nerve to touch her.

Wasting no time, I kicked in the door. I didn't look back to see if Reaper and Snake were with me. I knew they would be.

Thomas Williams was on top of Oya. Her clothes were ripped, and he had her dress pushed up to her waist. One of her eyes was swollen, her legs were scrapped up, and she had a busted lip.

He scrambled off of her and I didn't hesitate. I put a bullet in one of his knees so he couldn't get up and move.

"Get Oya out of here," I shouted as I stalked towards the congressman who was rolling around on the floor screaming.

"Gavin!" Oya shouted and my attention jerked to her.

The relief in her eyes calmed some of my anger, but not enough to let him walk out of here. Congressman Wiliams would die today.

"Go with Snake sweetheart."

She looked at me for a moment, then nodded. I think she knew what was coming next and there was nothing she could do to stop me. And I didn't believe she wanted to stop me anyway.

"I'll call a prospect," Snake said, "have them come get her with a cage, and take her to the clubhouse."

"Make sure Doc looks her over."

He nodded.

"Oya! Please, don't leave me," he begged.

"Shut up!" I yelled, pulling the trigger, and shooting him in the other knee.

She didn't turn around as Snake guided her out of the room.

· · · • · • • • · ·

It didn't take long for Reaper to tie the congressman to the chair that was located in the room despite his knees being shattered by my bullets.

"What do you have planned?" Reaper asked.

I held the barrel of the gun against my lips as I glared at Thomas Williams deciding how I could make him suffer. I was ready to get back to Oya to make sure she was all right.

"I should just put a bullet in his skull so I can get to Oya, but I want to make him suffer."

Reaper walked over to him and yanked his head back by his hair. Williams groaned but his eyes remained closed.

I walked over to him, then dug my finger into one of the bullet holes in his knees. He screamed and started to struggle against his restraints.

"You thought you could touch her!"

"I can do what the fuck I want to do to her. I'll fuck her in every hole if that's what I want to do because she's my fucking wife."

I gripped him by his neck and squeezed. "She's not yours, motherfucker." I squeezed tighter. His eyes started to bulge, and it was hard to explain the satisfaction moving through me. I'd only killed one time before this. I wasn't a cold-blooded killer and the last man I killed deserved to have his throat cut just like this piece of shit deserved everything that would happen to him.

"If I could prolong this shit, I would." I squeezed harder. His lips were started to turn blue and the tiny blood vessels in his eyes had started to pop. "But I've got to go take care of my woman. Not yours. Mine."

"Just go ahead and put him out of his misery, little bro," Reaper said, propped up against the wall.

I focused back on the congressman who was still struggling against his restraints. I let his neck go and he gasped trying to push air back into his lungs. I aimed my gun at his crotch and his eyes widen. He furiously began to shake his head. It was amazing he was more worried about losing his dick than his life. It wasn't like he was going to be alive to use it.

I pulled the trigger and the echo of the gunshot moved through the building only muffled by his screams of pain.

I aimed the gun at his head, and it didn't matter if he saw it coming or not. It didn't matter because he'd be dead anyway. "See you in Hell, motherfucker."

At the last minute, his eyes shot to mine, and I winked as I pulled the trigger, the bullet piercing his skull.

"I'll call King so he can get Messina to clean this mess up," Reaper said, pulling out his phone. "You did good, bro. Now go to your woman and I'll take care of this."

I nodded and headed out the door. It was done. It was over, now I only hoped Oya could live with the fact that I'd killed the father of her child. I didn't regret it and if I had to do it all over again, I'd still send that motherfucker to Hell.

CHAPTER FIFTEEN

"Do you need anything?" I asked.

It had been a couple of weeks since we got Oya back but I was still having a hard time dealing with what happened. She said she was fine, but it was hard to accept it when I saw how bruised her body was.

"No, I don't need anything." She smiled. "I'm fine. Stop worrying so much."

"I can't help it."

She gently kissed my lips. Before I could deepen the kiss, the television caught both of our attention.

Taylor, this has just come into the news center. This is breaking news from the police department. Oakland PD has announced the death of Congressman Thomas Williams. According to reports, the congressman has been found dead from an apparent drug overdose at a local motel in downtown Oakland, California.

Oya gripped my hand, but her eyes remained transfixed on the screen.

According to Oakland Police officials, Congressman Williams was found deceased today along with an unidentified female at a local hotel.

She gasped, gripping my hand tighter.

The police are approaching this investigation carefully, but initial reports are that both Congressman Williams and the unidentified woman apparently died from a drug overdose. An employee of the hotel who doesn't want to be named, and who allegedly found the bodies has told our very own Manny Cruz that the room where the congressman was found was littered with condoms, alcohol, drugs, and drug paraphernalia. The lead detective on the case said they will be making no statements until they've notified the next of kin. We will provide you with an update when we learn more.

I turned the television off. I wondered how Messina was going to handle Williams' body. He must have paid the police and coroner off because there was no way in hell those bullet holes could have been covered up without pockets being padded.

"Did you do this?" she asked.

"No. A Sinner's associate made it look like an overdose. Once I killed him, I went to you."

"So, nothing's going to happen to you?"

I pulled her into my arms, then hugged her tightly, kissing her forehead. Since I told her that I had killed him, she'd been terrified

I was going back to prison. I tried to reassure her everything was under control, but she had a hard time believing it.

"Nope. You're stuck with me," I said trying to break up the sullen mood. I didn't want her worrying about me, but I couldn't say that it didn't make me feel so fucking good that she cared.

Her cell phone rang, and she sighed. "That's probably Andrew," she said, standing up.

"Give him my condolences."

She arched her brow.

"He was an asshole who deserved to die, but that's still his father."

Of course, I wasn't going to miss the motherfucker and I did what I needed to do but I wasn't that much of an asshole that I couldn't feel sorry for his son. Who just so happens to be a good fucking guy.

She nodded and walked towards the kitchen.

I laid my head back against the couch and closed my eyes. Shit had been non-stop with the shop, Oya, and the club. We hadn't had a break in a long time. Maybe I could get Oya to go on a vacation. We both needed a break.

My phone buzzed and I opened my eyes, picked it up, and groaned when I saw the message from Reaper. I tossed the phone back on the table just as Oya sat back down on the couch beside me.

She squeezed my thigh. "What's wrong?"

I sighed. "Just got a message from my brother. My Ma wants us all at the house in the next few minutes."

"Is anything wrong?"

"Probably something dealing with my father. It always has something to do with him."

"Drew asked a ton of questions, but I didn't tell him what happened."

I nodded. Something had been weighing on me since everything happened. I needed to know if she wanted this to continue. She was my everything, but I needed to know if her feelings changed for me since I killed him.

I knew she cared for me. I didn't question that. But I did kill her ex, no matter the circumstances. I needed to know if she could deal with that. Would she still look at me as the same person?

"Are we good?"

Her brows pulled together, confusion covering her face. "Why wouldn't we be?"

"I need to know that your feelings for me haven't changed, Oya. I killed him."

She crawled into my lap, straddling my thighs. I palmed her ass through the fabric of her flowery dress. I looked deep into her eyes, inhaling the scent of her skin.

"I want to know that you can accept me for the person that I am. I'm not the good guy of this story Oya, which I think you know by now. Well, at least I hope you do. I've done some terrible things in my life, none of which I regret. This is who I am. A Sinner is what I'll be until the day I die. Can you handle that?"

For a moment I believed she was going to say no. She was an upstanding individual, the complete opposite to the tattooed biker ex-con but I couldn't deny the look in her eyes. Even if we hadn't said it to each other yet, she loved me as much as I loved her. I hadn't pressured her to say the words and she hadn't pressured me. It could be we both didn't want to get hurt, or run the other person away. But there was no doubt what I felt in my heart. This woman was my other half. I loved her.

"I can handle it," she whispered. "You are who you are Gavin. And I wouldn't want you to be anyone else."

My mouth crashed into hers. Our tongues warred. This was one thing I loved about Oya. She was an independent, dominant woman. She'd eventually give me her submission and let me take control, but she didn't give it readily.

Her hips rocked against my erection as I sucked her plump bottom lip before biting it. She hissed and I licked the sting. I pulled away, gripping her hips as she still rocked against my hardened length.

"You know I love you, right?" I asked.

Her movements still and her eyes widened.

I chuckled and pecked her lips. "You don't have to say it back. I just needed to tell you. Shit in this life can get hectic. Shit can go down so quick that you're not prepared and may not have the chance to do things and say things that need to be said. So, I want you to know that I love you, Oya Williams."

The smile that crossed her face lit my entire world up. Feelings assaulted me that I never believed I would ever feel. I don't know if I never felt worthy of someone, but I knew I didn't feel worthy to have someone like her. But I made the vow to myself to make this woman happy until the day I died.

Chapter Sixteen

I stood beside Oya, stoic. No emotions showed on anyone's faces except our Ma's. King was here with Alana, and Reaper comforted Ma. Today I was numb. It was the only way I could describe the feeling encompassing me. I wasn't happy and I wasn't sad that this day had come. Everyone was born to die. This day was just inevitable.

I can't say I didn't love my father because I believe I did. I just didn't like him. He was a terrible father and an even shittier husband.

When I was younger, I had an unconditional love for him. For both my parents. It didn't matter what he did, or how he treated me, he was still my Da, and I needed him to be better not only for himself but for us. He just never cared what any of us thought. He never cared to be that better person for us or for himself.

The clouds hung heavy in the skies. I hoped it would rain so it would give us all an excuse to leave. None of us wanted to be here except our Ma. But we all made the decision to show up, so she didn't have to go through this alone.

I watched as she tossed a red rose on his shiny black casket before they started to lower it into the ground. Thank fucking God it was about over.

When we found out he had lung cancer despite what he had done, I couldn't say that I was happy. My brothers were happy. They believed Karma was a bitch and he got what he deserved for how he had treated our mother and especially for doing what he had done to me.

I couldn't agree or disagree with that, but I knew that everything worked out how it should have. Me being there that night my father assaulted someone changed my entire life. Changed the person I was. I couldn't, in good conscience, say it was all bad. I was a business owner and if it hadn't been for prison, I wouldn't have that business. And if it weren't for Forbidden Ink, I'd never met the woman who has stood by my side regardless of all the things that would normally make a woman run.

She accepted me for the man I was. She accepted the Sinner. So, even though my father was a piece of shit, something good had come out of it.

Oya squeezed my hand pulling me from my thoughts. I caught sight of my brother and Alana leaving. I knew he wouldn't stay here longer than he needed to be here.

We understood each other a little better now since I told him what Da had done. Even though the heavy weight of that secret was finally lifted, where our relationship went from here remained to be seen. I'd like to have one and I believed so did he. All we could do was wait to see where it went.

"Are you ready?" she asked.

Every time I looked at this woman, I was reminded how lucky I was that she was here. She could have told me to go to hell especially after I killed her ex, but she stood beside me. And that was something I was grateful for, and I'd never forget or take it for granted.

I looked at my mother. She was wrapped in Reaper's arms, tears streaming down her face. I hated to see her so distraught over him. Regardless of what he put her through she loved him. Had loved him since they were in high school. I felt for her. I could sympathize because my fucking heart would be shattered into a little thousand pieces if I were in her position.

"Let's go say goodbye to, Ma. Then we'll head out."

Oya intertwined our fingers as I led her over to my brother and my Ma. Before her, I would have shied away from holding hands, hugs, or any public displays of affection. However, when I was with her, I needed the constant connection. She indulged me and sometimes initiated the connection before I had the chance.

When we reached my mother, she lifted her head from Reaper's chest and embraced me.

"I'm glad you came although I would have understood if you didn't."

I pulled away from her. "I came for you, not him."

She sighed. "I didn't know he had done that to you. I wished you would have said something when it happened. I'm sorry."

"We're going to head on out," I said, ignoring her apology.

Back then I didn't think she would have believed me, and I still don't, but now wasn't the time to talk about it. He was dead and what was done couldn't be changed.

"I love you, son."

I love you too, Ma. Call me if you need anything."

She nodded with tears in her eyes, and we walked away.

I hadn't forgiven my father and I wasn't sure I ever would, but I had made peace with what happened. And now that he was gone, I could truly let that part of my life go and move on.

I looked at Oya and smiled. I had a brighter future ahead and I couldn't wait.

Epilogue

WHAT A FUCKING WAY to wake up. I groaned as Oya's tongue ran up my dick along my Jacob's Ladder, from the base to the tip.

"You know this is going to make us late, right?" she asked.

I groaned when her tongue swirled around the head of my dick.

"He can wait," I said, as soon as her mouth engulfed me.

We were supposed to meet Drew for breakfast this morning. Apparently, he wanted to introduce his mother to the woman he was dating. Oya said it had to be serious because he never introduced anyone to her unless he believed it would last. She was so excited.

I gripped her locs, wrapping my hands in them and guiding her mouth further down on my dick until she gagged.

"Fuck, your mouth is fucking glorious. You take my cock so good, sweetheart."

She moved back up and I pushed her head back down until the pierced tip hit the back of her throat causing a shiver to move through me.

She grabbed my balls, then scraped her nails across them. I hissed from the sharp pain. "Fuck, babe. Do that again."

She scrapped her nails along my nuts again and my orgasm shot through me so quick. I groaned, pushing her head further down on my erection.

"Goddamn it, Oya," I moaned as I released in her mouth.

I closed my eyes, relaxed as I tried to catch my breath. She settled beside me, and I pulled her into my arms, then kissed her forehead.

"That was amazing. How about you wake me up like that every morning?"

She laughed. "I wouldn't mind it. It's the only time I get a little control in the bedroom."

She tossed her leg over my body and the peace and contentment I only felt with her encompassed me.

A few years ago, I never believed my life could be like this. Until her. When Oya walked into my shop three years ago my life changed. I wasn't one for complaining. Shit happened the way it happened for a reason. But now I believed I went through everything I'd gone through to prepare myself for the woman who was cuddled up beside me. The woman who had shown me love, without asking for shit in return except for my love. Without that struggle, without that time in prison, I wouldn't have been prepared for someone like her. She had her shit together. And she pushed me every day to have mine together too. I would forever be grateful to whoever or whatever sent her into my shop that night.

"I love you, sweetheart," I said.

She looked up at me with those beautiful brown eyes and like the first time I'd met her time stopped. She was my everything.

"I love you too."

Milton Keynes UK
Ingram Content Group UK Ltd.
UKHW020745231123
433129UK00017B/1189